Pigeon

Illustrations by
《 LINDA SUDHA BRACANOVICH 》

Throne

Written by

((BABA HARI DASS))

© 2009 by Sri Rama Publishing
P.O. Box 2550
Santa Cruz, California 95063
sriramfoundation.org

Production and editing by Prem Dass
Layout Designed by James J Guertin
First printing, 2009
10 9
ISBN 978-0-918100-26-9
Library of Congress Catalog Card No. 81 51052
SRI RAMA PUBLISHING is a non profit organization founded
to produce the writings of Baba Hari Dass.
Profits from the sale of books
and recordings are used to support Sri Ram Orphanage
in northern India.

CONTENTS

INTRODUCTION

Thousands of years ago in ancient India there lived an honest and righteous king named Karuna Nidhi. He and his lovely queen, Lakshmi, had a son whom they called Sundar, which means beautiful. Karuna Nidhi was the sole monarch of India, which had its capital in Ayodhya.

Prince Sundar was so beautiful that everyone in the kingdom wanted to see him all the time. So, to please his subjects, the king made a separate house for Sundar. In the center of the house there was a huge dome, the top of which was made into a room with walls of glass. Every morning Sundar would sit in this glass room so that the people of the kingdom could see him from long distances away.

At night the prince would leave the dome and go to his bedroom to sleep. His bed was made of sandalwood, and nine carved sandalwood pigeons held the bed on top of their heads.

Prince Sundar had many maid servants attending to him throughout the day. They were ordered to feed him, to wash and dress him, to put him to sleep with their songs, and to escort him to and from the glass room. He did not like having so many servants because their presence interfered in his play with some secret friends. So, one day, he requested his father to take all the maid servants away, saying, "Only one servant to bring me food is enough."

The king was very surprised to hear Sundar's request and said, "My son, you are so small. How will you do everything by yourself? And besides, these maid servants of yours are the most beautiful and talented musicians in the kingdom. I engage them only to serve you."

The prince said, "I can do everything by myself. One servant to bring me food is all I need!"

The king said, "All right, if you want only one servant, then select one, and the rest will work in the palace." The king thought that after some time Sundar would change his mind. The prince, though, would not even let the one maid servant attend to him. In fact, whenever she would bring him his food he would take the food and tell her to leave and to shut the door behind her.

Several days passed and Sundar was very happy without the maid servants. The king and queen however were worried. The queen thought that her son was going crazy, that he was sick, or that some demon had possessed him. But every time they went to the prince's room they found that he was happier than ever. And so they said, "If the prince is happier this way, then we should not bother him. We will not worry about him any longer."

So saying, they left for the palace.

The nine carved sandalwood pigeons holding up Sundar's bed were actually nine fairies. When there was no one else in the room, the pigeons would turn into fairies and talk to Sundar. They would feed him, wash him, and play with him. At night when the prince had a hard time going to sleep, they would turn into fairies and lift the bed high up in the sky. There it would float about gently while the fairies would tell Sundar stories. When he fell asleep, they would gently bring the bed back down to his room.

One night a fairy told a story about a very greedy king.

CHAPTER ONE

A Greedy King

Once upon a time there was a king in Bengal who was very greedy. One day he ordered that no one could stay in his kingdom unless they worked. It just so happened that in the kingdom several saints were living in temples. When they heard that they would have to work all day, they thought it would be better to live in the jungles. There they would be free to meditate as much and as long as they wished. So, all the saints left the kingdom and headed for the jungles. There they began to live in caves, under big trees, and in small huts.

Early one morning the king decided to go hunting. He had never hunted in his life and had never even seen a jungle. Taking a few of his chiefs with him, he went into a very dense jungle where there were many kinds of animals to hunt. The animals, though, were so fast that before the king could put an arrow in his bow, they would disappear into the bushes. Chasing deer and pigs, the king and his hunting party went very deep into the jungle. Spending the whole day in this way, they became hungry, tired, and thirsty, and sat down in the shade of a huge banyan tree to rest.

After a short time, they noticed a saint collecting firewood nearby. The king went over and kindly asked the saint for something to eat. The saint invited them all to his hut. He gave them water to drink and showed them a clean water pond where they could take a bath. The king and his party went to the pond with their horses. After bathing themselves, they rode their horses into the pond, bathing them as well.

They returned to the hut and asked for food. The saint walked forward holding a large pitcher filled with cheese. The king, who was not used to being without food for so long, was very hungry. He liked the cheese very much and asked the saint where he had gotten so much delicious cheese.

The saint showed him a cow that was grazing nearby and said, "This cow gives so much milk that I make cheese every day. And I don't have to do anything for her. She goes by herself for grazing in the morning and returns by herself at night. I put a can under her and she fills it with milk."

The king, with greed now overtaking his mind, began to think of taking the cow away with him. Not wanting to ask the saint to give up his cow, he secretly told one of his men to drive the cow away. Meanwhile, the king, in order to distract the saint, began to praise him for his hospitality and kindness and even invited the saint to visit him at the palace. The saint listened peaceably to the king and accepted his invitation to visit the palace. The king and his party then happily left.

When the sun went down and the cow did not come home as usual, the saint became worried. Even so, he sat down and began to meditate on his cow. In his meditation he saw the king and his men taking the cow away. The saint knew that the king was very greedy and decided to teach him a lesson.

After a few days had passed, the saint left to visit the king's palace. When he reached there, the king pretended not to know him. The saint very calmly reminded the king of his recent visit. He recounted the king's request for food, his bath in the pond, being fed cheese from a pitcher, and of the king's invitation to visit the palace. The king at once said, "Oh yes, I remember now. You live in a small hut in the jungle."

The king, who never thought the saint would take him up on his offer to visit the palace and, feeling uncomfortable in the saint's presence, said, "Well, I am very busy now, what can I do for you?"

The saint replied, "Oh nothing at all. I did not come here to ask any-thing of you. I have only come here to let you know that I have hundreds of cows like the one your men stole from me. And, as I am not needing them anymore, I am giving them away to anyone who wants them."

The king, although having just been called a thief, could not see through the greed that was again welling up in his mind. He immediately jumped up off the throne saying, "Don't give your cows away to others! Give them to me! I am your king!"

The saint, a faint smile visible on his face but acting surprised at the king's excitement, said, "Oh! well, yes, you can have them. I need just one cow for myself, so all the rest are yours." The bait being swallowed, the saint, now wanting to ensure that he got his original cow back, said, "And by the way, oh king, all of these cows give much more and sweeter milk than the cow your men drove away."

The king replied, "Good, I'll be there in seven days to bring them back to my palace."

The saint happily said, "All right, but remember, I'll need one cow for myself."

The saint returned home. He did not really have any other cows. He wondered what to do. Immersed in thought, he began to recount the inter-change that took place in the palace. Suddenly, he became aware that sev-eral rats were running around. In the twinkling of an eye, he changed them into beautiful cows. Thereafter, every rat he saw he changed into a cow.

Meanwhile, early on the morning of the seventh day, the king set out with some soldiers and a few cowherds in the direction of the saint's hut. As planned, the king felt the saint still had all the better cows, and, being the greedy king that he was, he decided to take the stolen cow back to the saint and to bring all the better ones to the palace for himself. When the king's entourage got near the saint's hut, they saw many beautiful cows grazing all around.

The saint saw the king coming with the cow he had stolen on his first visit and, pretending to be disappointed, said, "Oh king, why did you bring this cow back? I was wanting to keep the best cow for myself."

The king, feeling especially proud of his cunning, disguised his pride and said, "Sir, I took away your cow without asking you. It was stealing. It was not right. Now I bring her back. And, as you said that I can have all the cows except one, you keep your old cow and I'll take all the rest." So saying, he ordered his people to take the cows away. The servants at once rounded up all the cows, save the first, and drove them back toward the palace.

When the king reached the palace, he was beaming. He said to his people, "Now there will be no shortage of milk in the palace." The servants, ministers, and attendants cheered. The cows were then led to a huge barn near the palace.

The very next morning, several big cans were taken to the barn for milking. When the doors were opened, not one cow could be seen. Instead, hundreds of rats were seen running around.

The servants quickly informed the king that the saint had come secretly in the night and had taken all the cows away. The king became very angry and, together with his army, went straight to the jungle to arrest the saint. But, when they reached there, neither the saint nor any of the cows could be found. The king returned to the palace and ordered his soldiers to search the entire kingdom saying, "Find this thief and arrest him!"

In the meantime, the rats from the barn had gotten into the palace and destroyed all the clothes and linens, and spoiled all the food. There were rats everywhere. The queen, maid servants, and the children all left the palace in fear of them.

The king became even more upset because the rats were now attacking the people and their numbers were growing very fast. He could not think of a way to get rid of them. Despondently, he sat down near the barn. Then, he immediately jumped up, remembering that he, too, was afraid of rats. At that very moment a boy came running toward him. The boy gave the king a letter addressed to him and disappeared.

The king read the letter that said, "Oh greedy king, the rats will soon destroy your whole kingdom. If you want to save your kingdom, then distribute your wealth to the poor. In the future, whenever you feel greed overpowering your mind, remember this experience, and don't ever be greedy again."

The king realized his greed had caused the destruction of the palace. He had nowhere to turn; he could see no way out. So, trusting the message of the note, he distributed his wealth to the poor with an open heart. Henceforth, the rats disappeared from the palace.

Thereafter, the king realized it was the saint who had saved his kingdom from destruction, and who was instrumental in helping him realize that greed was the cause of misery. The king, who never forgot this experience, was never greedy again.

One night when all nine fairies had lifted Sundar's bed high up in the sky and it was floating about there, Sundar said, "I am not falling asleep. Do you know another story?"

One of the fairies said, "Yes, I know a story about an ignorant king. Listen..."

CHAPTER TWO

An Ignorant King

*L*ong, long ago there was a king in central India, in a province named Magadha. He was very big and very strong, and he had a long beard and mustache. Everyone was afraid of him except his ministers, who knew that the king, though big in body, had very little understanding. The king ate, slept, and played with his children. In actuality, the ministers were the real rulers. They were very cruel, dishonest, and cowardly.

The king's name was Gyan Dev. He had no knowledge about his kingdom. Whenever he would go outside the palace, his subjects would hide, and the markets would become empty. This happened because the ministers looted, killed, and imposed harsh taxes in the name of the king. The people did not know that all these tyrannical deeds were being done by the ministers. The ministers, for their part, would show much love to people whenever they would go out to inspect the different villages. The people would tell their miseries to the ministers. They would curse the king and sought the ministers' help in getting rid of their cruel king.

None of the ministers of King Gyan Dev was brave enough to take over the kingdom and become king because each was afraid of the other. So, together they decided to keep Gyan Dev as king and to make as much money for themselves as possible regardless of the means employed to attain it.

The neighboring kings heard about the pitiful condition of King Gyan Dev's subjects. They thought that he must be a very powerful king since his subjects were so afraid of him and never dared to revolt against him.

Except on the day when he got married to a beautiful princess of Assam, King Gyan Dev rarely left the palace. He never fought a battle, went hunting, or met any other kings.

His wife, the eldest daughter of the King of Assam, was brought up with several brothers who were strong and expert in the art of battle. So, naturally, she was also very brave and wise. King Gyan Dev was so much in love with her that he would not leave her for a second. She was his whole world. The queen also loved the king, but she could not understand how the kingdom was being ruled since the king did not even go to the high court with the ministers. She also noticed that she was watched by secret guards all the time.

In a short amount of time she had given birth to five children and she had little time to find out if the people of the kingdom were happy or in distress. Several times she asked the king about their subjects. He boasted that he ruled so strictly that no one ever dared to approach him directly. The queen tried to contact the ministers, but they told her that the king had given strict orders that ministers and high officials were not to go near the queen. They said he didn't want his beautiful queen to be seen by his servants.

One day the queen thought, "I am Queen of Magadha and here I am living in this palace like a female pig. I eat, sleep, and give birth to children. In seven years of married life, I have five children. I have not even gone out to see the kingdom one time. My life is no better than that of a prisoner. I was born in a family that is famous for its bravery. I was brought up with my brothers who are brave, skillful horsemen, and are expert in the art of battle. I used to stand in competition with my brothers on even ground, and here I am, sitting in my room, taking care of children, like an old maid servant."

The queen became very upset and depressed to see her condition. She

went to her husband and said, "I've never visited my parents since the day I got married. For two to three years after my marriage my brothers used to visit me and now they no longer come. I am very eager to see my mother. Would you take me to my parents' kingdom? If you don't want to go, then write to my father and he will send one of my brothers to take me."

The king said, "Darling, how can you go there? We have five children. I can't leave the kingdom. Do you know how much I love you? I don't even go to see my subjects outside. I don't want to leave you for a second."

The queen said, "If you don't go to see your subjects, then how can you tell if they are happy or in pain? You are not the real ruler. I am afraid some day your ministers will take over your kingdom and put you in jail. Then you couldn't see me or the children. Probably they will kill me and our children too!"

When the king heard this, he was shocked and frightened. He ran to his ministers and said, "I want to see my subjects! I want to see if they are happy!"

The ministers were very cunning and said, "Sire, your subjects are very happy and very respectful of you too. They don't even want to stand in front of you. They think their shadow will make you impure. If you want to see how much they respect you, then we can take you to the closest town."

The king said, "All right, I am going to change my robes. Prepare my horse immediately."

The ministers said, "Sire, you should go in a palanquin so that people will be able to see you from their roofs and balconies."

The king rushed to his room and began to dress. The queen was there and said, "Where are you going?"

The king said, "I am going to see my subjects. Do you know how much they respect me?"

The queen said, "How can I know without seeing them myself? I don't even know if there are people living in your kingdom. Maybe you don't have any kingdom. Maybe this palace, you, your ministers, me, and our children are your whole kingdom."

The king said, "Oh, do you really think that I am not a real king? Today I'll show you my kingdom. Get ready."

The queen became very happy and immediately dressed herself and her children. She took no time in getting ready. She was afraid the king might tell the ministers she was coming and that they would somehow find a way to keep her from going. The king was still in his dressing room when the queen came out and ordered the prime minister to get one palanquin ready for herself and another one for her children.

The ministers, as the queen had guessed, had not wanted the queen to accompany them. But now that she was all dressed up, they did not dare tell her she could not go. Instead, they went to the king and said, "Sire, the queen wants to go to see the subjects. Do you know that the queen is the most beautiful woman in our kingdom? If we take her outside, probably some evil eye will destroy her beauty. In our opinion the queen should stay in the palace."

The king said, "Oh no, no! I don't want the queen to get the evil eye. She may get sick and who knows, she may get possessed by some demon. I'll tell her to stay home. Where is she?"

The ministers said, "Sire, the queen is all prepared and ready to go. She ordered us to prepare two palanquins, one for herself and one for the children."

The king rushed out and found the queen and the children standing outside on the porch. He at once said, "My beloved, I am afraid to take you.

You are so beautiful that any evil eye can catch you. If you don't believe me, then ask these learned ministers." The ministers nodded their heads.

The queen became suspicious and said, "My beloved king, you told me that you will show me your subjects and now you are making excuses. Do you know I am married to you and I am your queen? The people have a right to see the queen of their kingdom. As for the evil eye, you should not worry. I am a daughter of the King of Assam. In that country magic is very advanced. All citizens know how to protect themselves from an evil eye. Do you see this amulet on my neck? No evil eye can affect me or my children as long as I wear it."

The king said, "Oh, you are right. No evil eye can affect you. You can go with me." The ministers' trick did not work. They could not say anything because the king was very impatient to leave and to show his wife his subjects. He started yelling about preparing palanquins and came out in the open yard where the palanquins were kept. The servants, when they saw the king standing in the yard, rushed forward with several palanquins. The king sat in one. Then the queen put her children in one palanquin and sat in another by herself.

As soon as the ministers rode ahead on their horses, the palanquins were carried away by the servants. Several soldiers and army officials also followed the ministers.

The ministers arrived at the market of the town. The people were not aware of the king's coming so they stood around on the roadsides. The ministers saw the people standing around and making noises. So, one of them galloped quickly ahead and yelled, "The king is coming! The king is coming!" As soon as the people heard that the king was coming, they ran to their houses and closed their doors. The stores began to close and, in a few minutes, the whole market became deserted. The king stood up on his palanquin and said, "See my beloved? See how much my subjects respect me? They don't want their shadow in front of me, and so they have left."

The queen said, "We can head back to the palace now. I have seen your subjects. No one checks each rice seed in a pot to see if it is cooked or not. If one rice seed is cooked, the whole pot of rice is cooked. If one seed is uncooked or half-cooked, then the whole pot is uncooked or half-cooked."

The king did not understand what she meant, but he was very happy that he could show his power over his subjects to his wife. He said proudly, "As you wish, my darling." He then yelled, "Let us go back to the palace. The queen doesn't want to go any further."

All the palanquins returned to the palace. The king was very happy. The ministers were feeling victorious. The children, though, were not very

enthusiastic about going back so early. The queen appeared very peaceful, but inside her heart she was very upset. She did not say anything to anyone but left for her room with a smile on her face.

Now the king became even more dependent on his ministers. The ministers started squeezing more money from the people by imposing more taxes. The taxes collected from the people would go in the ministers' pockets and not into the treasury. The people were in so much distress that many left for other provinces.

After a few days, the queen told her husband that he should take a look at the laws, the treasury accounts, and the taxes imposed in his name. The king never knew that he should check anything. He said, "Oh, I don't need to do that. My ministers do exactly what I tell them. I trust my ministers. They would not betray me. And, as you have seen with your own eyes, my subjects respect me. They are quite happy. So why should we worry about anything?"

The queen realized that the king was not only fat in body, but fat in his mind as well. He didn't know how to rule. She guessed that probably the reason their subjects were so afraid of him was that the ministers were very cruel, that he was getting blamed for their evil deeds. She decided to somehow save her husband from the clutches of his evil ministers.

She had a pigeon that she had brought from her father's house. The bird was a trained homing pigeon. Her father had used them to send letters from the battlefields to his queens. He gave one pigeon to his daughter in case she wanted to send a letter to him in an emergency. The queen wrote a letter to her father using a few symbolic words:

EMPTY PITCHER THIRSTY PEOPLE HELP

She put her seal on the paper and tied it to the pigeon's leg and released it from the cage. The pigeon flew high up in the sky and disappeared.

It was the summer season. The pigeon flew to the north. It flew for several hours. When it was tired and thirsty, it flew down and sat on the branch of a huge mango tree. A saint was living under the mango tree. Sitting on a different tree branch were a few wild pigeons that the saint would feed every day. The saint threw some grain in front of his hut and poured water in a big basin for the pigeons to drink and bathe in. All the pigeons came down to the ground and began to eat the grain. The queen's pigeon was also hungry and it came down and began to eat with the others.

The saint saw a new pigeon and looked at it curiously. He noticed something tied to its leg. He thought that maybe some bird trapper had tried to trap the bird and that, in getting away, it had gotten something tangled up in its foot. To rescue the pigeon from the knot, he gently caught the pigeon and took off the string that was tied to its leg. In doing so, the paper fell to the ground. Picking up the paper, he released the pigeon into the sky and it took off toward the north.

The saint read the paper and noticed the seal of the Queen of Magadha. At first he could not understand the meaning. Then he realized that it was the king who was worthless or empty, and that his subjects were the thirsty ones. He thought the message could become an invitation to some other king to attack. If so, then definitely several people would get killed in the battle. So, he put the note in his bag and decided to protect the kingdom from battle. He immediately left for Magadha.

The saint knew all the roads, towns, and villages of Magadha because he had been born there, and had worked there as a school teacher for several years. Growing older, he left his family and became a monk. He had been a monk now for several years. His hair was long and matted, as were his beard, mustache, and thick eyebrows. He was all gray. He had nothing on his body except a loincloth. He carried a small bag on his shoulders and a water pot in his right hand.

The monk went to the town closest to the palace. He begged food to eat and stayed in a temple. He saw the people were very poor, very thin, weak, and sickly. He asked the people if there was a famine in the near past. The people only whispered, fearing someone would overhear them. They said, "Revered sir, by the grace of God we get plenty of harvest every year, but everything goes in taxes. We can hardly get enough food for a full stomach. The king is a very cruel man. If someone is unable to give taxes, his soldiers beat him to death or burn his house and take away his wife and daughters. If anyone doesn't obey his orders, he will be burnt alive. Many people left this kingdom, many got killed, and we are all lamenting our own fate."

The monk did not take much time to understand the whole matter. He was a learned man. He had a sharp memory and all scriptures were on his tongue. He decided to meet the king, and he left for the palace. When he reached the gate, he was stopped by a guard. When the saint said he wanted to meet the king, the guard took him straight to the prime minister. The prime minister respectfully bowed to the saint and asked whether he needed money from the king, or if there were some other reason to meet the king.

The saint was very smart. He very humbly said that he was not only a monk, but a poet too, and that he wanted to sing his poems in front of the king. The prime minister said, "Oh, so you want to sing your poems to the king to get money." He took some money and put it in his bag.

The saint said, "I don't want money." But the prime minister only turned his back and told the guard to take him out of the palace boundary. The saint tried to force his way into the palace, but the guards dragged him out of the gate.

The saint went back to the temple and began to think of some way to meet the queen. All of a sudden, a thought struck his mind. If he should sing the words of the message at night near the palace, the queen would surely recognize it and try to find out who the singer was.

The sun hid behind the mountains and the birds flocked to the trees, making noises in getting to their proper places. The servants in the palace lit lamps in the rooms, on the palace path, and above the balconies. The saint went slowly from the temple toward the palace. The birds settled down in their places and stopped making noises. The servants finished their duties and went home. Everywhere there was silence. The saint walked close to the palace and climbed on a hill. He sat down on a rock and started singing with his beautiful voice:

"EMPTY PITCHER THIRSTY PEOPLE
PIGEON GAVE THIS MESSAGE
HELP-HELP-HELP"

He was absorbed in singing when the queen heard a melodious voice. She opened her windows and heard the code language she had sent to her father. She thought that probably her father had sent someone with a message for her. She immediately sent her maid servant to bring the singer into the palace.

The saint came into the palace, but his coming was not hidden from the eyes of the ministers. They surmised that there must be some secret plan going on. They all collected together and decided to kidnap the saint and arrest the king early in the morning.

The queen asked the saint what he meant by the song he was singing. The saint took out the message showing her own seal. He said, "I got this message from a pigeon and realized that if another king intercepted the message, he probably would come with an army and there would be a battle. To save innocent people from being killed, I decided to come and solve the problem peacefully."

The queen said, "Sir, the king has no power over his ministers. He thinks he is ruling the kingdom, but he is not. The ministers are very cruel and are torturing and harming the people in many ways. There is no other way except to get some help from outside to arrest these ministers and change the whole governing system. You can help me now only by informing my father. He would have sent my brothers had the pigeon been able to give them the message."

The saint said, "Oh, I see I have made a mistake then. I'll go to your father's kingdom at once. Please, give me a fast horse and I'll proceed right away."

The pigeon meanwhile had reached the kingdom of Assam. It sat down at the palace exactly where it used to live. The king saw the pigeon and recognized it. He saw there was no message tied to its foot. He became worried and thought that his daughter must be in a great crisis and did not even have the time to write a message. He immediately ordered his oldest son to go to Magadha with the cavalry to get a message from his daughter. The prince was a brave man. He at once marched with his horsemen toward Magadha.

In the palace, as the queen was talking to the saint, the king overheard some stranger's voice. He went into the queen's room and with a strong voice said, "Who are you to come into the palace at this hour?" He yelled, "Ministers, there is someone here. Come quickly!" The ministers were already hiding outside with several soldiers. When they heard the king's voice, they rushed in and arrested the saint. Then the prime minister, with a crooked smile, turned and said to the king, "Now sire, ready yourself to go to your new palace...THE PRISON! Ha Ha Ha. You are a worthless king. Your subjects are dying in miseries. They always complain that you should be removed. Therefore, by the wish of the people, we ministers have decided to imprison you. We proclaim ourselves as the rulers of this kingdom."

The soldiers chained both the king and the saint and took them out of the room. Now the prime minister laughed more softly and said, "Most respected queen, for you we have selected a very decent prison. Your beauty and the king's attachment to you made the king useless for his people. Therefore, you also deserve to be punished."

The soldiers rushed to arrest her, but she yelled loudly, "Don't come a step further!" She took her amulet in her hand and said, "This amulet will destroy you if you touch me!" The ministers had no courage. They stood as if turned to stone and could not decide what to do. In the meantime, the palace was shaken by the noise of galloping horses. In no time, the Prince of Assam, with several soldiers, entered the palace. The queen recognized her brother and screamed loudly, "Help the king! He has been taken to the prison with a saint. These cruel ministers will kill him!"

The prince sent a few soldiers to the king's rescue. He then arrested the ministers and directed his soldiers to take them to the prison. The next morning all the ministers were taken in chains to the streets. The saint informed the people that it was the ministers, and not the king, who had ordered the people to be tortured and beaten. And, as their rule was now over, they would get the same treatment they had given to others.

King Gyan Dev was very ashamed of having been a worthless king. He was ashamed that he had not been capable of protecting himself and that he had to be rescued by his brother-in-law. He at once proclaimed the queen the ruler. He then renounced the world and left for the jungle to live out the rest of his life.

The queen ruled the kingdom so well that her subjects became very happy, very strong, and were always very faithful to their dear queen.

Sundar became attached to the stories of the fairies and said, "Oh fairies, why don't you tell me a story every night before I go to sleep? I love your stories."

The fairies said, "Sundar, we know lots of stories. One of us will tell you a story every night."

The next night a fairy said, "Tonight it's my turn to tell a story. I know one about a magic bangle. Listen..."

CHAPTER THREE

Magic Bangle

Once there was a boy living in a village. His parents died when he was seven years old. The boy started collecting fallen wood from the jungles to sell in the town of Haridwar. In this way he began to earn his livelihood. When he grew older, he bought an ax and began to cut trees to sell in the market. He was then able to earn more money and he was very happy.

The boy grew into a young man and bought new clothes and cooking utensils for himself. He also repaired his hut, which was falling down.

One day, early in the morning, the wood-cutter went to the jungle and selected a big tree to cut. He thought that if he cut the whole tree and chopped it into pieces, then he could carry the wood to his hut and store it there. People could then come to his hut to buy the wood and that would save him from carrying it into town.

While he was chopping the tree, he found it was hollow inside. He was very disappointed and stopped cutting. But then he thought, "To finish cutting this hollow tree is better than starting to cut another one." So he started chopping again. As soon as he struck the tree with his ax, he heard a noise. It sounded like a piece of metal falling down. He looked inside the hollow of the tree and saw a shining golden bangle. He at once took it out and put it on his arm. As soon as he put the bangle on his arm, the young man felt that he was no longer a wood-cutter. Instead, he felt he was a learned man. He stopped chopping the tree, dropped his ax, and went home.

He said to himself, "Cutting wood and selling it in the town is a job for illiterate people. I should not be doing this kind of work. I am a wise man.

I should go to the king and, by my wisdom, show him that I should be his minister."

The wood-cutter took a bath, put on new clothes, and then went straight to the king's palace. No one stopped him. No one asked him where he was going. When the king saw a young man, whose face was shining like the disc of the full moon, standing in front of him, he stood up and said, "Young man, who are you? How did you come here? What do you want?"

The young man said, "My name is Satyawan. I was born in a village of your kingdom. I came here to show you my wisdom so that I may be your minister."

The king said, "You are still a young man. You need much experience before you become a minister. But I feel you are a learned man. I'll first have to see if you are fit for the job. For the present, you can have a place in my palace where all the learned people of the country are staying."

The next morning the court started. All the learned people, ministers, and generals took their seats. The king said, "Oh my courtiers, tell me how this month will unfold." The ministers and learned people all said good things to please the king. The king became very happy. Then he asked Satyawan if he could see anything either good or bad within the present month.

Satyawan replied, "Oh king, I can tell the future. But I don't want to make you happy by saying untrue things. If you really want to know the future then I can tell you privately."

The king dismissed the court and asked Satyawan to stay. When everyone had left Satyawan said, "Sire, your chief minister was not at the meeting."

The king replied, "Yes, he has taken leave for seven days to visit his relatives."

Satyawan said, "Sire, believe me. Your chief minister will attack your kingdom in exactly seven days. Half of the army is in his favor. If you want to save your kingdom then seek some help from outside."

The king angrily said, "You stupid boy! What are you talking about? My chief minister is a most honest and trustworthy person. Are you trying to turn my mind against him so that I'll give you his post? You are a beautiful young man and I thought you were a wise person, but now I see you are a crooked man. I'll give you a good lesson." He ordered Satyawan imprisoned for seven days. After seven days, the court would decide his fate.

The king went to his room and lay down on his bed. He began to think, "Although it is not possible that my chief minister will betray me, still I should be prepared for any danger. Who knows, perhaps the young man can see the future. I cannot tell the future, and this is why I need others to guide me. I asked him to tell the future and he told me what he saw. If he is trying to trick me, then he will surely be punished!"

The king very secretly sent a messenger to his brother, who was also a king, to post his army outside of his kingdom to help in case anything bad happened.

On the seventh day the chief minister came back to join his duties. He bowed to the king and raised both his arms in praise of the king. This move was a signal for the army. It at once surrounded the palace and captured the king, his courtiers, and all the others, and put them in prison.

The king's brother who was waiting just outside the kingdom, heard this news and at once attacked. The chief minister was not yet in control, so when the attack from outside came, there was no chain of command set up and he was not able to defend or to fight. The king's brother was at once able to surround the palace and capture the chief minister and his followers. He released his brother and the others from prison and took the chief minister away to his own kingdom to give him proper punishment.

The king then realized that what Satyawan had said was true. Actually, Satyawan had saved his life. He became very happy and proclaimed Satyawan his chief minister. The king also arranged the marriage of his beautiful daughter to Satyawan and gave them a beautiful palace in which to live.

On the advice of his new chief minister, Satyawan, the king made several reforms in his kingdom. This pleased his subjects very much.

A few years passed. The king became old and wanted to select one of his sons to rule the kingdom with love. He had two sons. The older son was brave and strong, but not very kind. The younger son was wise, kind, loving, and a poet, but he was not very strong.

The king's older son was afraid of Satyawan because he thought that Satyawan would recommend his younger brother for the throne and that the king would accept the advice.

One day the older son asked the king to allow him to go to the jungle to hunt lions. The king was happy to see his courage and said, "Yes, you can go, but take a few people with you."

His son said, "Father, Satyawan is my age. He is a very wise person and he is my close friend. Can we go to the hunt together? I don't need several people with me."

The king said, " Yes, Satyawan also needs some free time for recreation. You both can go together."

Satyawan heard the news that he was going on a lion hunt with the older son of the king. He did not want to kill lions, but he did want to travel in the jungle and look at the trees, birds, and animals. Not taking any armaments with him, he followed behind his brother-in-law's horse.

The prince thought, "If I kill Satyawan, then no one can stop me from becoming the king. But if anyone finds out that I killed him, my father will banish me from his kingdom. If I take Satyawan to a place where there are

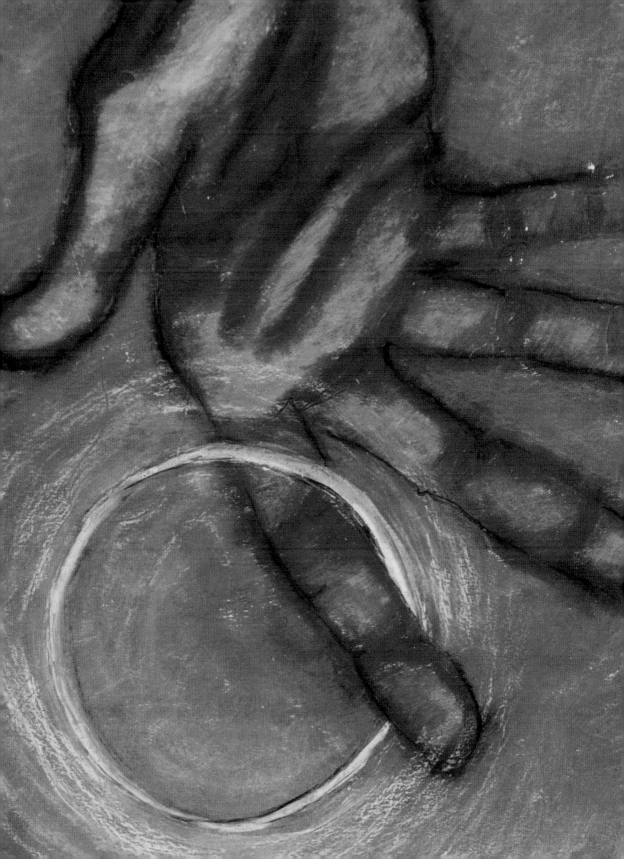

lions and a lion kills him, then no one can blame me." So the prince rode off deep into the jungle and Satyawan followed him, watching the birds and animals.

All of a sudden they heard the roar of a lion. Both horses jumped up, threw their riders, and ran away. Satyawan had no weapons and his brother-in-law's were tied to the saddle of his horse. Unarmed, they saw a huge lion standing in front of them. The prince was afraid. Satyawan saw the lion jumping toward the prince. He could not do anything except take off his golden bangle and throw it at the lion's mouth. The bangle went right into the mouth of the lion and was swallowed into its stomach! The lion bent his front knees and then lay down. The prince at once pulled Satyawan by the arm and they both ran away. Satyawan did not understand what was happening. He did not know where he was going.

When they returned to the palace, everyone was surprised to see them coming without their horses. The king called them to his room and the prince related the whole story. Satyawan remained silent. He did not know where he was, or who the king and the prince were. He had forgotten everything!

The king thought that Satyawan was in shock. He sent him to his home, but once there, he could not even recognize his wife. Several doctors checked him and could find no reason for the change. Satyawan's wife became very sad because he would say that his name was not Satyawan, that he was a wood-cutter, and that he was never married.

Everyone thought Satyawan had gone crazy. The king tried his best to revive his memory, but nothing helped.

One night Satyawan silently left his house and returned to his village. After cleaning his hut, he went to the jungle. He found his ax on the ground and saw the half-cut tree that had been left after he found the bangle. He started cutting the tree again.

He began to sell firewood as before. He totally forgot about the king, his becoming the chief minister, his marriage, and the lion hunt. He felt as if he had awakened from a deep sleep.

When Satyawan's wife found that her husband had disappeared, she became very sad and began to cry. The king also loved Satyawan and so he ordered his people to search everywhere for him. People left in groups and spread out in different directions.

The younger prince took a group of people to the jungles to search for Satyawan. They wandered in different places but could not find him anywhere. Finally, after much searching, they came to the same village where Satyawan was living.

Satyawan was leaving his hut. He put his ax on his shoulder and slowly went to the jungle to cut wood. The younger prince recognized him and decided to follow him at a distance. He did not want to scare Satyawan, but he wanted to watch his activities.

Satyawan went deep into the woods looking for a good tree to cut. The prince and his group saw him find a tree and begin to work. As soon as he struck the tree with his ax, a lion came out from behind a bush. The lion was huge but very thin and weak. He could hardly walk. When he came near Satyawan, he fell on the ground. Satyawan went up to him without any fear. The lion opened his mouth in an effort to vomit. Satyawan thought that something was stuck in his throat, probably a bone. So he put his hand in the lion's mouth. His hand touched something hard and he pulled it out. It was the same bangle he had thrown at the lion on the hunt. As soon as his hand touched the bangle, Satyawan's lost memory revived and he remembered he was the chief minister of the king.

When the bangle came out of the lion's throat, it stood up and leaped into the bushes and disappeared. Satyawan threw away his ax and put the bangle on his arm. The prince and his people saw all this and were very surprised to see that as soon as Satyawan put on the bangle he became a different person. They went to him and he recognized them immediately saying, "How is my wife? How is the king? I have to go and see them."

The prince took Satyawan back to the palace. When the king came to know that the younger prince had found Satyawan and that Satyawan's memory had revived, he became very happy.

He told his ministers to arrange a big celebration for Satyawan's return. In no time everything was arranged. At the celebration the king spoke thusly, "Listen, my subjects. I am getting old now. I had been wanting to select one of my two sons to become king for some time now. But when Satyawan disappeared, I decided that whoever found Satyawan and brought him back safely would be king. Fortunately for my younger son, he has found Satyawan and so now I proclaim him king!"

The younger prince had his coronation and became king. He ruled the kingdom with much love and through the years Satyawan saved him from many troubles created by his older brother.

⊸⊙⊸⊙⊸

The next night, when the fairies were swinging the bed gently, high up in the sky, one of the fairies said, "Sundar, I'll tell you a story of a cave man. Listen..."

CHAPTER FOUR

Cave Man

A long time ago, in the village of Kabul, a child was born so big that the mother could not deliver it and she died. The villagers, when they saw such a big baby, thought the baby was an incarnation of a demon. They told the father to take the baby into the jungle and leave him for the animals to eat. The father was also afraid. He believed the baby was really a demon, but he did not want to abandon him in the jungle. The villagers realized his love and attachment for the baby and said to him, "This baby is really a demon. First he killed his mother who gave birth to him. Next, he will kill you. Then he will destroy all of us. If you don't want to get rid of him, then leave the village and take him with you!"

The father said, "All right, I can't leave my village, my house, and my relatives. I'll get rid of him. I'll make a box to put the baby in, though, and then I'll throw it in the river. Either the baby will die of hunger or, if someone from another village takes him in, then he can destroy them and not us." The villagers thought this was a good idea and agreed to help. They made a box out of wood and put grass inside it. Over the grass they laid a sheep-skin. Then they put the baby in the box and threw it into the Kabul River, which empties into the Indus River.

When the box reached the Indus River, the baby began to cry from hunger. It was summer time. The day was hot, and the baby was getting the full scorching rays of the sun. His whole body became red with sunburn.

The Indus river is full of fish---big, small, and of different colors, shapes, and sizes. The fish smelled a human baby and tried to turn the box upside down. Sometimes they would jump up and make a splash of water. The splashes of water went into the box, wetting the baby and cooling his body. This saved him from the burning sun. Sometimes a small fish would jump right inside the box and land near the baby's hand. The baby would find it and suck it, as if sucking milk from the breast of his mother.

The box floated for several hundred miles and finally reached Sindhu, a province adjoining Bahlik, which these days comprise Sindhu and Punjab provinces. A fisherman there was fishing from his boat when he saw the box floating along. He moved quickly toward the box. He grabbed it only to discover, to his surprise, that a baby was in it. He tied the box behind his boat and rowed to shore.

He took the baby to his hut, where he lived with his wife and two sons, who were six and eight years old. The fisherman's wife liked the baby very much. She thought that when he grew up he would become a fisherman and be able to help her two sons.

She named the baby Dusyanta and began to take good care of him. Dusyanta grew very fast. Within a year, he was like a seven or eight-year-old boy. He never drank milk. He was brought up eating fish and meat. The fisherman and his wife were very surprised to see him growing so fast. The fisherman thought that if Dusyanta became a wrestler, he could get a very high post in the palace of the King of Sindhu, and then they would become rich. So he started feeding him excellent food, and taught him exercises and wrestling. In this way thirteen years passed and Dusyanta had grown to the size of an elephant. He was seven feet tall, and his chest was like a tree trunk. He would lift the boat by himself and take it to the river early in the morning. In the evening, he would carry the boat back to his village.

Once, while he was carrying the boat, the King of Sindhu, who was going fishing, saw this giant man carrying the huge wooden boat on his head. He asked the fisherman, "Who is this man?" The fisherman bowed to the king and said, "Reverend sir, this is a thirteen-year-old boy. I found him in a box floating down the river when he was just a baby." The king said, "Bring this boy to my palace tomorrow." And he left for fishing.

Next day, the fisherman took Dusyanta to the king's palace. Dusyanta had never been to a town before. When he saw all the people running here and there, like ants, he felt very uncomfortable and asked the fisherman if he could return to his village.

The fisherman said, "Dusyanta, we are going to visit the king. If we don't go, then he will punish us. If the king is pleased with you, then he probably will give you lots of things." Dusyanta said nothing and followed the fisherman.

They reached the palace. The king was sitting on a high, beautifully decorated throne. His ministers and generals were sitting on lower seats. When the king saw the fisherman and the boy, he addressed the boy saying, "What is your name?" The boy said, "Dusyanta." The king said, "I want you to live in my palace. You will be given much food and you will have nothing to do except exercise. I want you to be the strongest man in the world." Dusyanta said, "I don't like it here. I want to go home where I can swim in the river and play on the sand."

The king turned to the fisherman and said, "How much money do you want for him?" The fisherman very respectfully said, "Sir, we are your subjects. Our lives are for you. You can give anything you want."

The king said, "I will give you one village and you will leave this boy here." The fisherman bowed to the king several times and happily returned home. Now he was not a poor fisherman any longer. He was a rich landlord.

Dusyanta could not understand why he was being left behind, but when he tried to follow, the fisherman showed angry eyes to him. He had never done such a thing before and it caused Dusyanta to feel much pain. He also felt sad in the palace among all the new people.

Slowly time passed and Dusyanta became habituated to living among these people. The king had arranged a special diet for him, and two wrestlers trained him every day. Now he was in his full youth. He was so strong that he could knock down an elephant by butting it with one shoulder. He could grab a lion by its feet and, swinging it in the air, could throw it several meters away.

The king ordered his ironsmiths to make armor for Dusyanta out of steel with long spikes on the chest, back, and head. The armor was so heavy that it took ten people to lift it. But Dusyanta could put it on easily, and could also run and jump in it.

There came a time when the King of Bahlik invaded the kingdom of Sindhu over some boundary dispute. The King of Bahlik had a bigger army, and they were much stronger. They surrounded the kingdom of Sindhu and began to drive the people back. The Sindhu army could not stand for long. They all turned and ran for the fort. When the King of Sindhu found that his whole army had retreated and were hiding in the fort, he became very upset. He at once had the idea that if Dusyanta wore his armor and rushed at the enemy with his long heavy sword, then his own army would take courage and come out of the fort.

Dusyanta was ordered to go into battle. He put on his armor, took his sword, and in no time stood facing the enemy. The enemy attacked with their swords, lances, and arrows, but their arms were broken to pieces. If an elephant came forward to crush Dusyanta, he would dash it with his chest, and the sharp spikes would pierce the elephant's body.

When the Sindhu army saw that Dusyanta was crushing the enemy like ants, they got courage and came out of the fort. They sprang on the Bahlik army furiously and it was forced to retreat. The next day, again Dusyanta attacked the enemy army and drove it many miles further away. The King

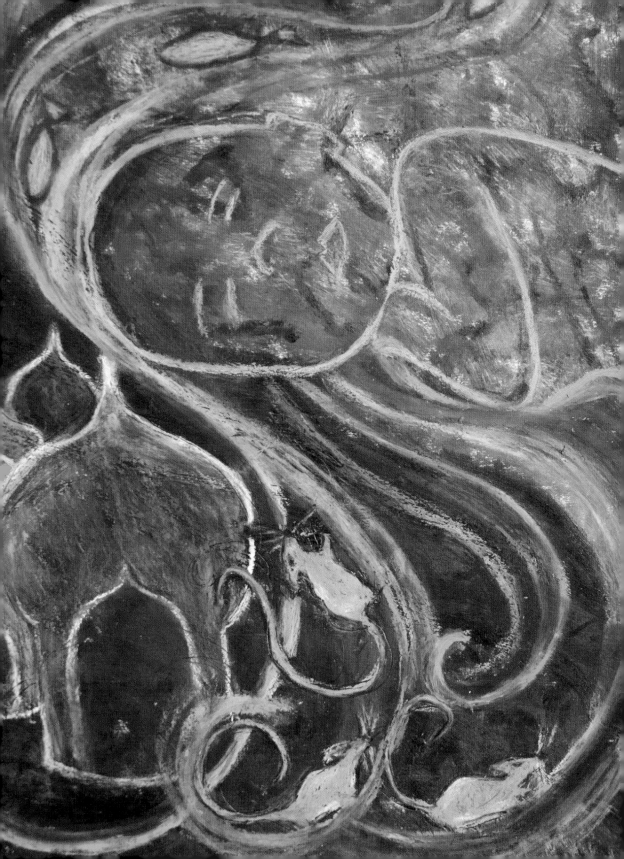

of Bahlik was in terror. There was no way to stop Dusyanta. Even the elephants were running away at the sight of him.

The Sindhu army finally drove the Bahlik army back to their own kingdom and surrounded their palace on all sides. The King of Bahlik was so disheartened that he threw himself onto his bed.

There was an old parrot in a golden cage hanging in the king's room. The parrot began to screech loudly making a noise, "RRRRRRat, RRRRRRRat." The king at once sat up and looked at the parrot. The parrot again and again screamed the same thing, "RRRRRRat, RRRRRRRat." The king called his minister. The minister came and, after bowing to the king, sat down with a sad face. The king said, "Bring a dozen rats immediately. Prepare a huge elephant. I'll go back into battle."

The minister arranged everything. The king put a long bamboo pole on the back of an elephant, together with a cage of rats, and he told his army to follow him.

When the king went to the battlefield, he saw Dusyanta coming toward him like a demon. He immediately took a rat out of the cage and tied it by its tail onto the end of the bamboo pole. When Dusyanta came near and was about to dash the elephant's head, he saw the rat! He jumped back with a scream! The king swung the rat and when it touched Dusyanta face, he was so terrified that he turned and ran away. The army of Bahlik, in the meantime, was attacking the Sindhu army. But when the Sindhu army saw Dusyanta running away, they also turned and followed him.

The King of Bahlik then declared victory.

When the King of Sindhu found out that Dusyanta had run in terror at seeing a rat, he was very ashamed. He called Dusyanta and said, "You can smash an elephant's head with one blow and yet you ran away, just seeing a rat. I don't want a coward like you in my kingdom."

Dusyanta did not say anything. He took off the clothes he had gotten from the king and left, wearing only a loin cloth. He did not know where to go or what to do. He kept walking, crossed the boundary of Bahlik and entered a dense jungle, which was the territory of the King of Ayodhya. There was a cave in this jungle by the side of a river. Dusyanta liked the place very much and began to live in the cave. The jungle was so dense that no human being ever entered it, so the animals and birds were not frightened. Dusyanta was very friendly to them. Elephants, tigers, lions, deer---all were his friends. The birds would sit on his head, hands, and shoulders. He was very happy away from the town people.

Several generations passed. Several kings ruled and died. Several kingdoms disappeared from the earth. Several new kingdoms were formed, but Dusyanta was still the same in his cave. His body was covered with long hair, and the hair of his beard, mustache, and head also grew very long.

The fairy said, "Sundar, when your father's great-grandfather started rebuilding the fort, which was falling down in various places, he found a huge man sitting outside a cave. When he first saw the man, he thought he was a demon; no normal human being could be so big. He also thought that maybe the huge man had come from some other planet."

The king said to his minister, "The area of my fort covers this cave. So as long as this demon, or whatever he is, is living here, we can't rebuild the fort."

The king ordered his generals to go to the caveman to try to find out who he was. Gathering their courage, the generals went up to the man, but they could not understand his language. He was talking in some very ancient tongue. They realized that he was not a demon and thought that probably he was from some other planet and was hiding there out of fear.

They informed their king that the caveman was not a demon; he was a huge man who talked in some ancient language. The king and the public came to see the strange man. Soon, thousands of people started coming and going all the time. The caveman, when he saw so many people, became very upset, and roared like a lion. Everyone was so frightened to hear his roar that they ran away. The king again said to his generals that as long as the caveman was not driven out, they couldn't rebuild the fort. But no one was willing to talk to him, even if they could have understood his language. So the king decided to send an army to either arrest him, or to drive him out of the kingdom.

When the army reached the area and surrounded the cave, the caveman remembered his past battle and he again roared very loudly. The army ran away in fear. The soldiers prepared a huge elephant to try to catch him. They tied ropes to the elephant and slowly rode closer and closer to the cave. The caveman was sitting peacefully outside when the soldiers threw a rope around his neck and started to pull the elephant away from him. The elephant stopped with a jerk. The elephant could not even drag the cave-

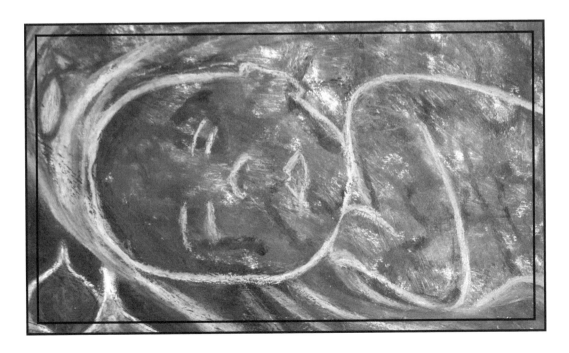

man a few feet. When the soldiers continued to order the elephant back, the caveman pulled on the rope dragging the elephant forward. The caveman untied the rope from around his neck and continued pulling the elephant toward him. When the soldiers who were riding on the elephant saw that the caveman had been able to pull the elephant forward, they were very frightened by the man's strength and, jumping down, they ran away.

The general then decided to send several elephants to fight with the caveman. Each elephant carried four soldiers. All the elephants attacked together. When the caveman saw the elephants coming toward him, he at once jumped to the top of the cave and rolled a huge boulder down on them. The boulder was so big that it dashed several of the elephants, and the rest ran away in fear.

The king thought that if he continued his fight with the caveman, probably his whole kingdom would be destroyed. So, the king stopped the war and changed his mind about making a fort around the cave.

When the war was over, everyone went to see the huge man near the cave. He then rolled a large boulder against the mouth of the cave and slipped inside. From the inside, he pulled the boulder tight against the opening of the cave.

No one ever saw the caveman again. After waiting for a few years, the king finally rebuilt the fort over the original place.

-o-o-o-

When the story was completed, Sundar fell asleep and the fairies brought him back to his room. In his sleep he was dreaming about the caveman with long arms, long legs, and hair all over his body. When the caveman rolled the huge boulder over the elephants, it seemed to be rolling right over Sundar's head, and he was very frightened and screamed loudly.

It was morning. The king, queen, and maid servants heard the scream and they ran to Sundar's room. Sundar was awake now, but he was still afraid. Before anyone reached his room a fairy secretly whispered, "Sundar, it was only a dream---don't be afraid!"

When Sundar saw his parents and servants come into the room he sat up and said, "I was dreaming."

His mother said, "Sundar, you were screaming. I don't want you to be alone. You were afraid. Tell me, what did you dream?"

Sundar said, "I was afraid. I felt something was falling on me; that's all. But don't worry, mother. I am alright. I don't need anyone in my room. I am happy like this."

The queen said, "If you are happy to be alone, then it's alright. But I am worried. Tell us any time you feel lonely."

Sundar said, "I don't feel lonely, Mother. I am fine." Everyone left Sundar's room. Sundar began to play with the fairies as usual.

One of the fairies said, "Sundar, you screamed so loudly in your dream that your parents and servants will now come here more often to see you. We can't play and talk with you as freely. If anyone comes, we have to hide inside the wooden pigeons. If we tell you stories, you dream the story and get scared. What should we do?"

Sundar said, "I'll not scream any more. Please, I like your stories. If you don't tell me stories, I'll... stop eating... I'll not go to bed... I'll..."

The fairies interrupted, "All right, all right! If you don't scream any more, then we will continue to tell you stories."

One of the fairies said, "This is a story about a crazy beggar who appeared in Benares. No one knows from where he came."

CHAPTER FIVE

Brown Blanket

Once, while some people were going to bathe in the river Ganges, they saw someone sitting in a corner resting his back against a wall. His head was resting on his knees and his whole body was covered by a blanket, which was dark brown and filled with dirt.

At first, everyone thought that some huge boulder had drifted away from the river sand somehow, and stopped at this corner. But when they came near, they saw a blanket and someone snoring inside it.

One person said, "Oh, it is a beggar, probably crazy. Let us go and take a bath before the sun comes up." The people took their baths and left. All day long, up to midnight, people came to take baths and no one saw the man lifting his head or changing his position. In this way, seven days passed. Everyone was very surprised to see a man sitting like a rock for seven days.

A few people said, "He must be a high saint." A few said, "Oh no, either he is crazy or he is a cheat." Some young boys pulled his blanket. The beggar slowly lifted his head and stretched his knees. Then he lay down on his left side, keeping his back toward the people.

The boys said, "Oh, he must be intoxicated by some kind of drug. Leave him alone." Everyone left.

When everyone had gone, the man again sat down as before. This time he covered his body with his blanket like a mummy, and kept his face uncovered. A few children were playing on the bank of the river, making paper boats. When all their boats had floated away down the river, they left for home. But when they saw the man's body covered by a blanket, one of the boys said, "Look at that man. He can be our horse. Let us go and ask him if he wants to play with us."

All the children ran up to him and said, "Will you play with us?" The man nodded his head. The children said, "You can be our horse. You are big. We all can ride on you, okay?" The man nodded his head. One of the boys put a rope in the man's mouth and said, "This is your rein and now we all will sit on your back. Walk on your hands and knees pretending you are a horse." So saying, all the children jumped onto his back, bashing into each other trying to find a good place to sit. The man neighed like a horse, and began to walk on the sand pretending to walk like a horse, sometimes fast, sometimes slow, and sometimes he would stop. When he stopped, the children would kick him and pull his rein to make him run.

It was great fun. The children played all day long and forgot to go home. When the sun was about to set, and the bells of the temples began to ring for evening services, they remembered that it was very late. They all jumped from the man's back and ran away to their homes.

The man stood up and shook his blanket. He stretched his back and went back to his place, and sat down again.

The pilgrims of Benares, who come to take baths in the river Ganges, give food to beggars. So when the man sat down, people gave him fruits, vegetables, rice, etc. He ate some and when everyone had left, he gave the leftover rice to the fish in the river.

The next day, the children came again and, without saying anything, they jumped on his back. The man pretended to be a horse all day long, and when the children left in the evening, he sat down again in his place.

Grownups saw him playing with the children, and when they went to talk to him, he did not reply at all. They said to each other, "What kind of man is he? He plays with children and now he is sitting like a rock. He is definitely crazy. The children should not play with him any more." And they all left.

He became the children's best friend. No one ever heard him talk. Even in playing, he would not talk, but only nod his head. He was a perfect horse,

and the children fell in love with him. Sometimes the children would fight to sit on his shoulders because the first rider would hold the rein and control the horse. Sometimes the horse would go wild and throw his hands and feet up and down and all the riders would fall, except the first one. He was able to pull the rein very tight by leaning backward, and then the horse would stop jumping.

Slowly the number of riders increased, and the children began to fight for their turns. One day, the man stood up and threw his blanket high in the sky and when the blanket came down on the ground, there were several toys to play with. For the whole day the children played with the toys and then they tired of them and began to throw them in the river.

A man was watching all this from the roof of his house far from the bank of the river. He saw the strange man throw the blanket up in the sky, and then he saw different kinds of toys underneath the blanket. He was very surprised and thought that the man was definitely a magician: probably he was doing all this in order to kidnap the children. He went straight to the King of Benares and related the whole story. The king ordered his soldiers to bring the man into court.

While the children were playing with the man, as usual, the soldiers surrounded him and one soldier said with a stern voice, "Who are you? From where did you come?" The man sat down like a rock. The soldier said, "You seem to be a very cunning fellow. You were playing with the children a few minutes ago, and now you are pretending to meditate. We know the tricks of rogues. Don't try to deceive us! Get up! We will take you to the king." When the man did not move at all, the soldiers took his blanket, wrapped him in it, then forcibly lifted him up and took him away to the court.

The king came to the court and asked the soldiers, "Who is he?" The soldiers said, "He doesn't talk. He was playing with the children and, as soon as he saw us, he sat down like a rock, just as he is sitting here." The king said, "If he doesn't talk, then take off his blanket and whip him on his bare back! Then he will reply!"

The soldiers lifted the man and took him to prison. They took off his blanket and put it on a table. Then a soldier came with a whip made of braided leather. He soaked the whip in water to make it more flexible and then with his full strength started whipping the man. As soon as the soldier started whipping, the brown blanket jumped from the table and came in between the soldier and the man. Not a single whip lash could touch the man's bare back.

When the soldier saw that the blanket was stopping the whip, he moved to the front. But the blanket also moved to the front, and when the soldier moved again to the back, the blanket also moved to the back. The soldier became very angry and began to run around the man very fast, but the blanket kept ahead of him. The soldier ran and ran, and at last became so tired that he fainted.

Then the man stood up with his blanket and walked out of the prison and disappeared. When the soldier came to his senses, he ran out and told the other soldiers that the man had escaped. All the soldiers were afraid because the king would punish them if he found out the man had escaped. So they went out on a search.

One of the soldiers said, "Let us go to his regular place. Probably he will be there." It was almost dark. Evening services in the temples had just been completed, and the pilgrims were leaving for their homes. The river bank was almost without people. Only a few boatmen were sitting in one corner smoking tobacco in their pipes.

The soldiers were a little afraid and so went to the boatmen first. When the boatmen told them to go to the dark corner where the beggar was living, one soldier said, "We want you to show us the place." All the boatmen stood up and slowly walked toward the beggar's corner, still smoking their pipes and continuing their chit-chat.

When they came close to the beggar, a boatman said, "Here he is! Now we are leaving."

The beggar was sitting very calmly, wrapped in his blanket, as usual. The soldiers yelled, "You rogue! Why did you run away from the prison? We will teach you how to talk! Do you know that we can extract oil from the rocks? Even the demons are afraid of us!"

Two soldiers grabbed the beggar by his arms, and the rest of them started to whip him. At the same time, the blanket unwrapped from around his body and began to swing, throwing sand in the soldiers' eyes, and pushing them away. The soldiers tried their best to beat the beggar, but they were never able to touch his body, even once.

When the soldiers saw that they could not overpower the beggar, they ran away. On the way, they decided to tell the king that the man was very bad, that he was a magician and a thief, and that he wanted to kidnap the children. They hoped that the king would order him to be killed.

The soldiers reached the court and one of them said, "Sire, that man is not really a beggar. He is disguising himself as a beggar but, in fact, he is a magician. With his magic, he charms the children and kidnaps them. He is also a thief. We tried our best to make him talk, but he wouldn't. When we went to eat our food, he secretly ran away and now he is sitting on the bank of the river. We tried to bring him back, but he threw sand in our eyes, and kicked, and threw rocks."

The king very angrily said, "Bring him to me. I'll see who he is!" The soldiers began to look at each other. They were expecting the king would say, "Kill him." Then they would have the choice of either killing him or requesting him to leave the kingdom.

The king yelled, "Why do you look at each other's faces? Bring the man here immediately!" The soldiers at once bowed to the king and went to the place where the beggar was sitting. They were afraid of him and so they crept slowly up to him, like cats. The man remained sitting like a rock, as usual. One soldier very peacefully said, "The king wants to see you. He wants to know who you are. Please forgive us for our rude behavior. If you don't go to the king with us, he will punish us!"

The beggar at once stood up and, without uttering a single word, went to the court. The soldiers followed him. When they reached the gate, the soldiers grabbed the beggar by his arms and began to drag him, trying to show that they were bringing him in by force.

They took him to the court where the king was sitting. When the king saw the soldiers pushing and dragging the beggar, he became very angry and yelled, "Bring him here!"

The beggar stood in front of the king very peacefully. The king said, "Tell me the truth. Who are you? Magician? Thief? Spy? Or are you trying to kidnap the children to sell them to other countries as slaves?" The beggar remained silent.

His silence increased the anger of the king so much that he jumped from his seat with a loud scream and drew his sword. He swung the sword at the beggar's neck so hard that the sword passed through the beggar's neck and spun the king around three times before he could stop its force.

Everyone saw that the blanket was standing, but with no head. The soldiers jumped to find the chopped off head on the ground, but they saw nothing. The king also checked the blanket and found that there was neither a head nor a body inside.

The king said, "Let us go and kill that rogue. He might be in his same place." The king and the soldiers ran with their naked swords, yelling and screaming, "Catch him! Catch him! Kill him! Kill him!" But they could not find him. At last, they came back very tired. Their voices were hoarse from screaming. When they got back to the court, they saw the brown blanket stand up. It flapped its corners, and then flew away into the sky. No one ever saw that man in Benares again.

As soon as the story was finished, Sundar began to snore. He fell asleep in one second. The fairies brought the bed back to the room and turned themselves into pigeons as usual.

In the morning the maid servant came early to see if the prince was still asleep. She quietly came into the room and as she was covering Sundar with his blanket, he woke up and said, "Fairies, what are you doing?"

The maid servant said, "Prince, are you dreaming? It's only me. There are no fairies here."

Sundar rubbed his eyes and smiled. He said, "I thought you were a fairy." The maid servant also smiled and left the room.

That night, after taking food and when his parents had left his room, the prince said to the fairies, "What will happen if my parents see you here?"

The fairies said, "Sundar, if anyone sees us and guesses who we are, then we can't live here any longer. We will have to leave and take this bed away with us."

Sundar said, "You will leave me? I wouldn't leave you. I'll always be with you."

The fairies said, "If we can keep our presence a secret, then we won't have to leave. But now we are doubting whether you will be able to keep the secret. Do you know, Sundar, that you will grow older, get married, and become a king? Certainly you will not care about any of us then."

Sundar said, "Don't say all those things... I get sad... Tell me another story."

One of the fairies said, "All right. Don't be sad. I'll tell you a story about a golden fish. My mother told me this story when I was little. I used to ask her to tell the same story every day. So I remember it word for word..."

CHAPTER SIX

Golden Fish

In the previous epoch there was a very kind, honest, and compassionate king named Lakshman Singh. His kingdom was in Ayodhya. The king would give alms to the poor every morning, and he ordered that all beggars and helpless people be offered food every day. He made water ponds for cattle to drink from during the summer, and he planted shade trees by the side of footpaths for people to sit under during the heat of the day.

His subjects were very happy and loved him dearly. The king was happy too, but he had no son to be the king after him. This was the only pain he had.

Once the king called together the intellectuals, astrologers, priests, and family teachers for a meeting. He said, "Listen, oh wise people. I respect you very much. You all know that I don't have an heir. I want you to suggest the most suitable person to be king after my death." The names of several young men were suggested, but none of them appeared quite fit in the eyes of the king.

The family priest said, "Sire, you are not very old. You can still have a child. If you agree, I will arrange a fire ceremony to please God and ask that God give you a child."

The king said, "Reverend sir, I give you full authority to arrange the fire ceremony. You can spend as much money as you want from the treasury."

The fire ceremony was performed by several priests over a period of three months. The king and queen attended it every day for six hours.

When the ceremony was completed, the queen found that she was pregnant. The news spread quickly and the whole kingdom became happy.

The queen soon gave birth to a baby boy. The baby was beautiful. The king was very happy when he heard the news. Now he had an heir who would become king after him. His pain and sadness were finished.

When the baby was a year old, the queen again became pregnant and gave birth to another boy. The following year once again she became pregnant and this time she gave birth to a baby girl. The king and queen were contented to see two boys and one girl in their family.

Slowly all three children began to grow. The older son's name was Vikram. He was calm, kind, and compassionate, and also extremely handsome. The second son's name was Indrajit. He was strong, brave, and firm in his determination. The girl's name was Jai Sri. She was beautiful and intelligent.

When Vikram was thirteen years old, the king sent him to a school far away from the city. All the students there lived like hermits in their small huts and studied scriptures, archery, horseback riding, wrestling, and other subjects.

Once in the evening when Vikram went to the river to fetch water, he saw a beautiful girl sitting on a large rock next to the wooden boat that he and some of the other students had made. He was surprised to see such a beautiful girl sitting there all alone and wondered how she had come to these woods. He went over to her and said, "Oh beautiful lady, how did you come to these woods? Our teacher is a hermit. He has no family and no one else lives around here except his students, who are all boys. You must come from some other place."

The girl said, "I live in a nearby village and came here walking along the bank of this river. We use the river to irrigate our land. Today I wanted to

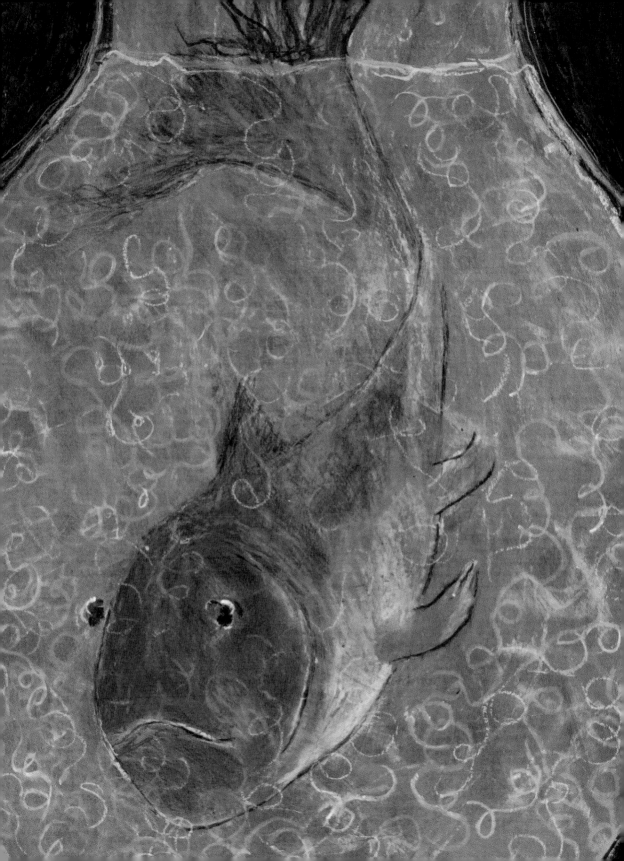

see how far the river goes, but I was tired and sat down here to rest. I'll go back to my home now, but first, tell me who you are."

The boy said, "My name is Vikram. I am a Prince of Ayodhya. My father sent me here to study scriptures, archery, and the skills of battle. In a few years I'll go back to my home."

The girl said, "Vikram, I am very happy to meet you. In my village there is no one my age and I often feel lonely. Can I come again in the evening to see you?"

Vikram said, "Oh sure. You can come." Looking at the boat nearby, Vikram said, "Did you know that boat over there is ours? My friends and I made it ourselves. Maybe one day we can go down the river in it. It goes very fast!"

The girl said, "All right. I'll come tomorrow," and she left for her home. Vikram filled his pitcher with water and went back to his hut.

The next day the girl came late. Vikram waited for her for a long time. She said, "Vikram, I am sorry I am so late. Tomorrow I'll come earlier." They talked for some time. They quickly became friends.

The following day the girl came earlier and took Vikram to visit a nearby village. The girl had fallen in love with Vikram but he had no idea of her love. He treated her like a sister.

One day the girl said, "Vikram, the river is so full and fast. Let us go out in your boat."

Vikram said, "Can you swim? The river has a pretty strong current. If the boat capsizes we will have to swim to the bank."

The girl said, "Oh, yes, I can swim. I was born near the bank of this river and learned to swim as a child."

Vikram said, "Then it's all right. Let's go." They both sat down in the boat and Vikram pushed it with the oar into the current. The boat began to float swiftly down stream. They enjoyed it very much.

The girl said, "Vikram, give me the oar. I'll turn the boat now toward the bank."

Vikram gave the oar to her and she began to turn the boat, but it slipped from her hands and was swept away by the current very quickly.

In the meantime, the small river had joined a larger one. The girl said, "Vikram, we can't swim this big river and we don't have the oar. What should we do?"

Vikram said, "At least this big river is not flowing with such force that it will capsize us. Somewhere along the way we'll reach the bank. Now, I want to rest. Will you watch the boat?"

The girl said, "All right. When the boat comes to the bank, I'll let you know."

Vikram stretched out his legs and put his head on the seat. He closed his eyes to rest, but he soon fell asleep.

The boat floated a whole day and night, and when Vikram finally opened his eyes he saw that the boat was on a shore. He said, "Now we are on shore. Let us walk to our home."

The girl said, "Vikram, we are on an island. I don't know how we reached here. After you fell asleep, I also fell asleep. It seems that we have drifted into the ocean and finally landed on this island. Let us go. I am hungry. I want something to eat." She jumped out of the boat and Vikram followed her.

The girl walked very fast along a trail, as if she was fully acquainted with the island. Vikram said, "Where are you going? We don't know anything about this place. BE CAREFUL!... Don't go so fast!"

The girl stopped, turned to Vikram, and said, "Vikram, listen. I know everything about this island. I live here. When I first saw you at the bank of the river I fell in love with you, and I put you to sleep in the boat to bring you here. Vikram, I love you. I want you to marry me. This whole island is ours!"

Vikram said angrily, "You tricked me! I am going back to my home!" He ran to the shore and found that the boat was not there.

The girl said, "Vikram, I love you. That's why I brought you here. Don't try to run away. You can't escape from this island." Vikram became very sad and followed her with heavy feet.

When the teacher did not see Vikram at dinner time, he was worried and told the students to search the woods for him. They searched all night but did not find him. In the morning a message was sent to the king about the disappearance of his son, Prince Vikram.

The king and queen were very upset to hear this news and went out with a search party of hundreds of people to find him. They looked in every area of the woods. Divers looked everywhere in the river. No trace of Vikram was found.

Alas, they finally declared that Vikram had been swept away by the flooded river and that he was no longer alive.

The king and queen returned home very sad. They began to carefully watch their second son, Indrajit, and their daughter, Jai Sri. The two children were not allowed to go outside the palace. Their teachers had to come into the palace to teach them.

Meanwhile, back on the island, the girl who had kidnapped Vikram was actually an evil witch. She had disguised herself as a girl in order to kidnap him. When she saw that Vikram was following her calmly, she became very happy and said, "Vikram, I am the princess of this island. I want to marry you. Look! There is my palace. Soon you will see how beautiful it is."

Slowly they came to the front of the palace. The witch held Vikram's hand and took him inside.

The palace was extremely beautiful. All the walls were made of carved white marble. The ceiling was made of gold plated copper sheets in different designs. Precious stones fixed in the ceiling were glittering like stars by the light of the lamps.

There were several rooms, all exactly the same. If anyone attempted to enter these rooms, it would not be easy for them to find their way out. The witch showed Vikram all of the rooms and then finally took him to her own room at the center of the palace.

It was completely round with a domed roof. The walls of the room were also made of carved marble but of different colors. They were studded with jewels. The domed ceiling was made of pure gold with pearls, diamonds, and other precious stones fixed on it.

In the center of the room there was a huge bed. The bed was not on the floor but was hanging by golden chains from the ceiling.

The witch said, "Vikram, this is our room This bed swings when anyone sits on it and it makes music. Let us try." They climbed onto the bed and when it began to swing, the melodious music of flute and veena were heard. The witch said, "Let us get down now; otherwise, we will fall asleep. We have much work to do."

The witch showed Vikram the garden, the lake, and the watch tower. Vikram said, "Oh Lady, you have such a beautiful palace and so much wealth, but no one else is here. What is the reason? Where are the people? Do you live all alone in this huge palace?"

The witch smiled and said, "Look! The herd of deer, the flocks of pigeons, the fish in the lake, the trees in the garden... Look! Those big rocks... All these are my friends. I don't need anyone else. I only wanted you, and you are with me now and I am very happy."

Vikram said, "I miss my parents. Take me home. They will be worried about me. I want to go home. I don't want to live here with you."

The witch was very much in love with Vikram and did not want to show anger, so she politely said, "Vikram, you have everything here. If you still miss your parents, then I'll take you home after a month. Be happy now. We have so many things to play with. We can go boating in the lake. We can run in the garden. We can sit on the beach and watch the ocean. We can play with the animals. We can sing and dance."

When Vikram heard that the witch would take him home after a month, he felt happier and began to play with her.

Slowly the time passed, and the witch became even more attached to him. She was afraid, though, that after a month he would ask her to take him home.

When the month had passed, Vikram, who had been counting each day, said, "Now a month is over. Let us go back to my teacher's place."

The witch said, "Forget your parents! Forget your home! This is your home! You are the king of this island! Live here happily with me!"

Now Vikram was very sad, but he did not say anything. He began to feel that this girl would imprison him forever on the island. He thought about his parents, his friends, and his brother and sister, all of the time. He decided to run away from the palace at night. He thought that if he saw a boat in the ocean, he could swim out to it and be saved.

One night, while the witch was fast asleep, Vikram woke up and very secretly crept out of the room. He ran toward the ocean.

As he was running through the garden he heard the noise of the trees flapping their branches and saying, "Vikram, don't try to run away. We are watching you!" Vikram at once stopped and realized that the trees were talking like human beings. He was frightened and turned in the other direction.

All of a sudden, a herd of deer crossed his path. They turned their heads toward him and said, "Oh prince, don't try to run away. We are the guards!" Vikram saw that the deer were actually human beings. Now he was very frightened, and he ran in another direction like a crazy man.

There was no trail. The ground was full of rocks. Vikram jumped over the rocks and came to a huge boulder. He tried to climb over it to get to the other side. As soon as he had climbed onto it, it began to shake and he heard someone laughing, "HA! HA! HA!" Vikram saw that the boulder was a huge monster's head. It angrily said, "Watch out! I am standing here. Don't try to run away!"

Vikram was terrified and now he knew that it was impossible to escape from this island, so he returned to the palace.

He secretly climbed onto the bed and saw that the girl was still fast asleep. He lay down by her side, but he could not sleep.

The witch was only pretending to sleep. She was awake and knew exactly what was going on, but she did not show it.

In the morning she said, "Vikram, you look tired. Didn't you sleep?"

Vikram said, "I miss my parents, my brother and sister, and my friends. That's why I can't sleep."

The witch stood up and pressed a button on the bed. A door opened in the floor. She said, "Follow me." She went through the door and down some steps. Vikram followed her. When they reached the bottom floor, it was totally dark. The witch pushed a button and the room became lit.

In the light, Vikram saw several boys his age hanging head down with their feet tied to the ceiling. The witch said, "Vikram, all these boys tried to run away from this island. Now they are hanging here. Don't try to run away again. Those trees, deer, and boulders are all my guards."

When Vikram saw so many boys hanging from the ceiling, his head began to spin. He felt light-headed and fainted. The witch carried him up to her room and laid him on the bed. When Vikram came to his senses, he saw the girl leaning over him, pressing his head.

She said, "Vikram, don't be afraid. I will give you one more chance. Within a month, make up your mind to marry me or else be hung in the dark room with the others. There is no other alternative."

Vikram closed his eyes in fear and did not say anything. The witch was so madly in love with him that she hoped to change his mind by scaring him. He was tired, and afraid, and he fell asleep. When he woke up, his whole body was sore. He could hardly move. The witch rubbed his body with oil and he felt better.

The witch said, "Vikram, I have to go away for three days. Don't try to run away. If you do, you will be killed by my guards. Remember, I love you and I want you to live here with me happily. I'll see you in three days."

Vikram found himself all alone in the palace. He was afraid to go outside and he was afraid to touch anything inside. He knew that the witch's guards were everywhere, and that in any place there could be a trap door.

Vikram remained in the bedroom for two days and became very tired and sad. He thought, "It would be better to die than to live any longer in this golden cage." This simple thought became stronger and stronger in his mind. He forgot about the guards and trap doors. He was no longer afraid.

Vikram left the palace and walked toward the shore. He had decided to swim as far as he could. When he reached the edge of the water, he jumped in and swam for a long time. There was a big fish living near the island. When she saw Vikram in the water, she came near and put her head between his legs and took him back to the shore.

At the touch of Vikram, the fish felt as if she was related to him in some past life. She said, "Vikram, I know why you want to leave. Don't be afraid of me. I am also a guard here but I will favor you. First listen to my story..."

I am a princess of the great King of Kamroop. The king was famous for his bravery and magical powers. He had no son. So, when I was born, he dressed me as a boy.

When I was three years old, the woman of this island kidnapped me thinking that I was a boy. When she found that I was a girl, she turned me into a fish. She also changes people into trees, boulders, and deer so that they will not be able to run away."

Then the fish whispered, "Listen, I want to get my human form back, but I can't do anything. The witch is so much in love with you that if you show affection for her, she will be very happy and will not harm you. And, I know a secret about her that can destroy her very easily and release us all from this prison! The witch keeps a key in her belt. That key opens a door on the north wall of the bedroom. First, you must find the keyhole on the wall and then, after making the witch happy, you can steal the key from her belt and open the door.

Behind the door you will find a jar made of glass. Inside the jar there is a golden fish. That fish holds the power of the witch. If you can take the jar before she finds out about the key, then you are saved. But if she knows before you touch the jar, then immediately she will change you into an animal, a tree, or a rock. Or, she will hang you upside down in her dark room.

I also tell you that once you take hold of the jar, the witch will scream with an awful voice and her real witch-body will appear. Don't be afraid of it because she loses all her powers as soon as the jar is in your hands. The witch's powers will then come to you and you can change all of us back into our real forms.

Vikram, I have told you the secret. Now I tell you again---be very nice and loving to the witch and when she begins to trust you, you will find the right time to do your work. Don't do it in haste. You will spoil the whole plan if you don't have patience. Now, before the witch arrives, go back to your room and try to be happy."

Vikram left for his room, and the fish dove deep into the ocean waters and disappeared.

When the witch returned, she found Vikram completely changed. He was no longer sad. He hugged and kissed her with much love. The witch thought that Vikram had changed because he was terrified at seeing the boys hanging upside down. She became very happy thinking that her trick had changed his mind.

Now Vikram pretended to be deeply in love with the witch, and he would not allow her to go anywhere without him. He asked her if she would marry him. The witch said, "We are married now. You are the king of this whole island, and I am your queen. You already know that these trees, deer, and boulders are human beings, so they will not frighten you any more."

Vikram began to live on the island as if he were happy. The witch trusted him so much that she stopped secretly watching him. They would play together in the room, dancing and singing songs.

One night while the witch was changing her clothes, Vikram saw the key hanging on her belt. He said, "Why do you keep that key with you all the time? Isn't it uncomfortable for you while you sleep? Let me see it."

The witch took off the belt and put it in Vikram's hand. Vikram said, "Is this the key to your treasure? You have not shown me your treasure."

The witch said, "My beloved, you will see the treasure some day, but now let us go to bed." She took the belt and hung it on a post of the bed.

Vikram said, "I love you very much. Now, I don't miss any of my family and I can't live without you. Sometimes I get sad when I think that you might leave me here and go away somewhere else."

The witch hugged and kissed Vikram and said, "No, I can't leave you. I love you. You are my life. Don't ever say that I will leave you!"

Talking for a long time about their love, they both finally fell asleep. Vikram dreamt that the big fish in the lake was whispering, "VIKRAM, DO YOUR WORK. DO YOUR WORK."

He at once woke up and saw that the witch was fast asleep. He silently took her belt and crept like a cat toward the north wall. He put the key in the hole and it made a noise, "R-r-r-r-..." A door opened.

The witch turned on her other side when she heard the noise of the key. She opened her eyes and saw a glass jar with a golden fish swimming in it, in Vikram's hand. She screamed loudly and turned into her furious witch form, but she could not move to get out of the bed.

The witch yelled, "You wicked boy! You tricked me! You showed so much love, but secretly you found out about the jar and the golden fish."

Vikram said, "Oh witch, you tricked me first. You kidnapped me as you have kidnapped so many others. Remember your sins. Your end is near!"

The witch began to cry and said, "Don't kill me, Vikram. You can have anything you want. Have mercy on me, please!"

Vikram said, "First I'll release all those trees, deer, and boulders. After that I will decide your fate."

He opened the dark room and ordered the golden fish to release all the boys who were hanging there. The fish shook her tail and the boys dropped to the ground and walked out of the room. Then all the witch's other prisoners were released.

Everyone collected in the round room where the witch was still screaming on the bed. When Vikram asked them what to do with her, they all yelled, "Kill her! Kill her!"

The witch was very frightened and begged for mercy. Vikram said, "Oh witch, you really loved me. Now your life is in my hands. I don't want to have to kill you, so please tell me how to send you away from this world."

The witch said, "Thank you, Vikram, for your kindness. Take this bed to the mountain top where there is a deep hole. By the use of ropes you can lower the bed inside the hole. When it touches the ground, I will disappear inside the earth."

Vikram told the people to take the witch to the mountain top. They lifted the bed onto their shoulders and carried it up the mountain. When they reached the top they put the bed inside the hole and slowly lowered it down. As soon as it touched the ground, a puff of smoke came up and sealed the hole forever.

Vikram returned to the palace and ordered the golden fish to send all of the people back to their homes. In no time the island was empty and Vikram remained alone.

He thought he should check everywhere to see if everyone was safely gone before he left. He looked around the palace, then the garden, and finally reached the shore. He found that the fish, who actually saved the lives of everyone, was swimming at the shore.

Vikram at once ordered the golden fish in the jar to bring the big fish back to her real form. Immediately the big fish changed into a strong and beautiful princess.

Vikram bowed and said, "Oh princess, you saved the lives of all the people captured on this island, including me. I am very grateful to you. Now I will send you back to your home."

The princess bent down on her knees and with folded hands and tears in her eyes, she said, "My lord, when I took you out of the water I touched your body. You are the first man I ever touched. I immediately realized that you are my husband from previous lives. If I go to my parents' house after so many years, they will not accept me. My life will be painful. Moreover,

I cannot marry anyone else, for I love you."

Vikram said, "When you saved me from the water, I also felt as if we were related in our past births, and I too am in love with you. If your parents won't accept you, then let us go to my parents."

Vikram ordered the golden fish to take them to his parents' palace in Ayodhya. As soon as they left the island, it sank deep into the ocean.

When Vikram and the princess entered the king's palace, the jar and the golden fish suddenly disappeared from Vikram's hand.

The king, the queen, and the whole kingdom became very happy when they saw Vikram alive. The king had the princess and Vikram married and Vikram became King of Ayodhya.

One of the fairies said, "Sundar, do you remember the big fish who was in the lake? The one who saved Vikram from drowning and was Princess of Kamroop? Her father, the King of Kamroop, was famous for his magical powers, but the witch was more powerful. As long as the witch had her power, he could not see the vision of his daughter. But, after the witch disappeared, the King of Kamroop saw in meditation that his daughter was in Ayodhya and that she was married to Prince Vikram. Let me tell you this story."

CHAPTER SEVEN

Bravery of Indrajit

The King of Kamroop became very angry because his daughter had married without informing him. He at once called his chief minister and said, "My daughter Jivanti is alive. She is my only child. She is in the palace of Ayodhya. Send some faithful soldiers to secretly kidnap her."

The chief minister bowed to the king and made a plan to kidnap Princess Jivanti. Four soldiers who were very intelligent and expert horse riders were selected to go to Ayodhya. They were to enter the palace somehow, and kidnap Jivanti unharmed. An army was also sent in case they were chased by the soldiers of Ayodhya while bringing her back.

When the plan was all set up, the four soldiers left and after some time finally reached Ayodhya. One of the soldiers remained outside the city with the four horses, and the other three went into the city disguised as traveling magicians. One played the part of the magician and one was disguised as his wife. The third played the part of a drummer.

Kamroop province was famous for its magic. Everyone there was a magician. It was their tradition to learn all magic tricks and perform them at festivals and other ceremonies.

So, the three disguised magicians began to show their magic at different places in the city. Everyone was amazed to see their tricks.

The king heard about the extraordinary magic of the foreigners and ordered them to perform their magic for the students in the palace school.

The magicians came to the school and started singing to the beat of the drum. Everyone sat down. Prince Indrajit and his sister Princess Jai Sri were in the center on a well-decorated seat. On each side of them sat the boys and girls of the ministers, generals, and other courtiers.

The magician put a basket on the ground in front of him and began to play his flute. Everyone was deeply concentrated on the flute.

Suddenly the flute and the drum both stopped and the magician, in his deep voice, said, "Look here!" He opened the lid of the basket. "There is a rope in this basket. I am taking out one end of it." He took out the end and turned it upward. Then he again began to play the flute.

After a while the magician's wife said, "Look! The rope is standing up like a snake lifting its hood." Everyone saw that the rope was really lifting up like a snake. The drummer increased his speed and the magician changed the tune of his flute. The rope began to rise faster and faster. After a few minutes it was standing straight up. Only one coil remained in the basket. It was a very long rope.

All of a sudden the drum and the flute stopped and everyone was in silence. The magician, in his deep voice said, "Now I'll climb up on this rope." Then he turned to his wife and said, "My darling, I am going into battle. Do not leave this place before I return." The wife hugged him and with tears in her eyes she said, "God is with you. I'll pray for you and wish you victory."

The drummer started drumming and the woman began to sing in her squeaky voice. The magician held a sword in his mouth and began to climb up the rope like a monkey.

When he had reached half way, he called out very loudly to his wife, "Can you see me?"

The wife called back, "Yes, I can see you. You are very little--about the size of a beetle." The people heard the voice of the magician coming from

very far away, and when they looked up, they saw him sticking on the rope just like a beetle.

When the magician's wife started singing again, the magician began to climb and the people's attention was drawn again to her song.

A few minutes later, from a great distance, the voice of the magician was heard, "Can you still see me? Now I am on top of the rope where it joins the battlefield!"

The woman yelled, "I can't see you any more." The people also looked up, but could not see the magician at all.

The drummer changed his rhythm and the woman began to sing a song about a battle. Everyone felt that a furious battle was going on somewhere in the sky. They had been very surprised to see the magician disappear, and now the noise of the battle frightened them.

They heard the sound of running horses and of soldiers yelling, "Kill him! Kill him!" Battle drums and bugles were sounding from both sides.

All of a sudden a human arm dropped down right in front of the magician's wife, who was very busy singing with her eyes closed. Then another arm fell. Then one leg, and another leg, and then a headless trunk all dropped in front of her. But the woman and the drummer were completely absorbed in the music and did not notice. The people saw all the limbs covered with blood, and they were terrified.

When a head fell down on the lap of the woman she opened her eyes and saw that it was her husband's head. At the same time the drummer stopped playing and the woman began to scream, "My husband is killed! My husband is killed!"

While all this was going on, the fourth soldier had come from outside the city. He saw Jai Sri sitting with Indrajit and he thought that she was the Princess of Kamroop. He secretly put some drugged incense on the table in front of her and it made her faint. In the confusion he quietly took her in his arms and carried her away.

The magician's wife was lamenting loudly as she put the arms and the legs back onto the body's trunk. Then she put the head on the neck and covered the corpse with a white cloth. With tears in her eyes she said, "Now I am going to the king to get money for the funeral services of my husband," and she left.

The drummer started drumming again and people saw that the corpse inside the cloth began to move. In a few minutes the magician sat up and said, "Where is my wife? Someone has taken her away. I must go to the king to complain that my wife has been kidnapped by his soldiers. My wife is kidnapped!" he screamed, and he disappeared.

The drummer stopped drumming and said, "Now the play is over." He pulled the rope into the basket and, leaving the drum and his bags on the ground, he said, "Now I'll go to the king to get my reward." He slowly walked away.

The bag, drum, and basket were left sitting there. Everyone thought they would come back after getting their reward and continue showing their magic tricks.

When Indrajit noticed that his sister, Jai Sri, had disappeared, he ran toward the palace to see if she was there. When he arrived, he found neither his sister nor the magicians. He guessed at once that they had played a trick and had kidnapped Jai Sri.

Without saying anything to anyone, Indrajit went to the stable and prepared his horse to chase the magicians.

No one in the crowd knew what was happening. Everyone was still mesmerized by the drums and magic.

The soldier who kidnapped Jai Sri took her away on his horse very fast.

After throwing away their magician clothes, the other three soldiers found their horses outside the city and followed the first soldier. One soldier, the drummer, stayed at a distance behind and was prepared to stop anyone who chased after them.

The fairy said, "Sundar, as my sister told you, Indrajit was very strong, and brave, and had firm determination. Do you remember?"

Indrajit was a very good horse rider also. He had the fastest horse in the stable. He and his horse were of the same age. They were both thirteen years old and were like brothers.

When everything was ready, Indrajit took his sword and jumped on his horse. In no time, he rode out of the city through the main gate. He knew immediately which direction the magicians would take.

While he was riding very fast, Indrajit saw dirt rising in the distance far away. He said to himself, "That is definitely the dust from some galloping horses." He tightened the reins a little and the horse began to run like a hawk chasing a pigeon.

When the soldier following in the rear realized that someone was chasing them, he turned his horse and galloped back toward Indrajit. He drew his sword and was prepared to attack. When Indrajit's horse came near, the soldier swung his sword toward Indrajit's neck, but Indrajit's horse was very smart. When he saw the soldier swinging his sword, he dropped down on his knees for a second and the sword passed over the top of Indrajit's head. Then he galloped away.

The soldier thought that he had killed the chaser. He stopped his horse and began to look for the body. He could not find any body or head, so he thought that probably the man was injured and his horse had taken him away in another direction.

The soldier got on his horse again and rode toward Ayodhya. He wanted to stop any more enemy soldiers right inside their kingdom so that his friends would have time to get completely out of the country.

Indrajit's horse was very fast. Indrajit was only a young boy and not very heavy, so his horse was not tired. The horses of the soldiers ahead of him, though, were tired, and their speed slowed down.

Again, very far away, Indrajit saw dust rising and this time he drew his sword to attack. The two soldiers saw him in the distance and thought that the fourth soldier, who had been staying behind, was coming toward them.

Indrajit's horse passed the two riders very quickly and in no time disappeared from their sight. The men could not recognize who was on the horse. They thought that it was probably the other soldier showing them that he had started last but could easily pass them. They did not care about it and continued at their own speed.

It was dusk and the sun was about to set. Now Indrajit's horse was also tired so Indrajit decided to stop somewhere for a couple of hours to give the horse a rest. While Indrajit was still looking for a place to rest, the two soldiers arrived. They were also looking for a place. When they saw the prince, they said, "Oh, so you were chasing us! Now be ready to die! The princess is far away. You can't save her."

Indrajit yelled, "You thieves! I could have cut your heads off when I passed you, but I don't want to fight. I only want the princess back. If you want to live in this world for a few years more, then tell me where she is!"

The soldier said to his friend, "This boy is threatening us. It's as if he were talking to the servants in his palace. Let's give him a good lesson!"

The soldiers rode forward until they were face to face with the prince. Indrajit's horse at once turned around and kicked one soldier right on the forehead. The man fell down to the ground, senseless. Then the horse quickly turned again and stood up on his hind legs and caught the other soldier's right arm with his mouth. In one jerk he broke the arm that was holding the sword. This soldier also fell off his horse and became senseless.

Indrajit tied both the soldiers to a big tree with the rope from their horses. He took off the horses' saddles and, pointing the horses toward Ayodhya, whistled loudly. This frightened the horses and they headed in that direction. He sat down under a tree and both he and his horse rested.

The fourth soldier, the one who had kidnapped Jai Sri, reached a place where an army of Kamroop soldiers was waiting for him. He changed his horse for a fresh one and, without taking a rest, rode with Jai Sri toward the kingdom of Kamroop.

When he felt that he was far enough away from Ayodhya so that no one could find him, he slowed down.

After a couple of hours the soldiers who were tied to the tree came to their senses and began to groan, "Water... Water." Indrajit poured water into their mouths and they opened their eyes.

The prince said, "Tell me the truth. Otherwise, I'll chop your heads off. Who are you?"

They said, "We are the soldiers of Kamroop. Our king ordered us to go to Ayodhya and bring back his daughter, Jivanti, whom you were hiding."

Indrajit said, "You idiots! You didn't kidnap Jivanti. You kidnapped my sister, Jai Sri!" The prince at once jumped on his horse and in a second disappeared from their sight.

The two soldiers said to each other, "We probably made a mistake and kidnapped the Princess of Ayodhya instead of the Princess of Kamroop! If the prince reaches the palace and the king hears about this, he will be very angry with us. Maybe he will even kill us. We should try to kill the prince before he reaches the king. The king will not know that the Princess of Ayodhya is not his real daughter since she was kidnapped when she was only three years old. After so many years, the king could never recognize her completely. And, if the kidnapped girl says she is the Princess of Ayodhya, the king will not believe her. He will think that she just wants to go back to her husband in Ayodhya. Somehow, we must free ourselves."

Night passed and it was morning. The sun was rising. The soldier who had followed behind slowly came riding toward the place where the other two soldiers were tied to the tree. When he saw them, he jumped from his horse and went near. He asked, "What happened? Who tied you to this tree?"

One soldier said, "The Prince of Ayodhya injured us and then tied us up here."

The newly arrived soldier said, "He was also chasing me. When I heard him coming up behind me, I turned my horse and ran toward him and struck him with my sword. Are you sure he was the Prince of Ayodhya? I thought I killed him. At least he was gravely injured."

The soldiers said, "Oh, no. He is not injured at all. Release us and we will tell you the rest of the story."

The soldier released both of his friends and sat down beside them. One of the soldiers said, "We have made a great mistake. Instead of kidnapping the Princess of Kamroop, we have kidnapped the Princess of Ayodhya. When the prince reaches the king and tells him the whole story, he will be very angry with us. But if we can kill the prince before he reaches the palace, we will get a large reward from the king for bringing back his daughter."

"If you ride quickly ahead," he said, looking to the soldier who had rescued them, "and meet our army, then you can send two horses back for us and take a few other soldiers with you to catch the prince."

The soldier said, "If that be the case, then I should not wait here a second longer. I am going. I'll send two horses back for you." He leaped onto his horse and galloped away.

The army of Kamroop was moving very slowly, waiting for the three soldiers, thinking that if they got any news of fighting they might have to go forward to help.

Indrajit's horse was so fast that in no time he was within sight of the army. Indrajit saw the army from a distance and recognized them by their dress. He stopped his horse and thought, "It is stupid to fight with an army single-handedly. Even if I get out alive, much time will be wasted in fighting. I will bypass the army by going through the jungle." The prince pulled his horse from the trail and rode into the jungle.

The jungle was very uneven with hills, valleys, rocks, and rivers. It was also full of lions, elephants, and snakes. In some places there were swamps, and in other places inaccessible hills.

There was no trail and Indrajit had no idea where he was going, but he was determined to bring his sister back. After riding for a long time he knew that he was lost. He began to feel that his horse was his only protector---his guide and friend.

They headed through a valley and continued to go deep inside the jungle. On both sides there were high mountains. A river was flowing very quickly through the valley. Indrajit did not know if he was ahead of the army or behind it. But his horse walked on very cautiously.

Suddenly a sharp arrow darted in front of Indrajit and his horse shied and stopped. Then from the bushes several men jumped forward with lances, swords, bows and arrows. The men were very dark and their bodies were painted with white stripes. They were tribal people who captured people from other tribes, and sacrificed them in front of their goddess.

The tribals surrounded Indrajit on three sides and made a way for the horse to walk. They were screaming and dancing with happiness. Indrajit had never seen tribal people before, and he did not know what they wanted to do.

They reached an open plain with a mountain on one side. At the bottom of the mountain there was a huge rock carved into the figure of a woman. This was their goddess, and she was decorated with human skulls.

By signs, they communicated to Indrajit to get down. They took his horse away. The prince did not want to leave his horse, but the men forcibly led him away and put Indrajit in a very deep ditch with bamboo poles on the top. They dropped some bananas inside the ditch for him to eat.

Indrajit realized that he was imprisoned and he was very worried about his horse. He knew that these were mountain people who did not know anything about horses, and might feed his horse bananas and leaves.

The next day the tribals sat together and talked about sacrificing Indrajit and his horse at midnight, in front of their goddess. When the sun had set they started drinking alcohol and began to dance.

The horse still had the saddle on his back and the reins in his mouth because the tribals did not know how to take them off. They let the horse roam free because for them he was like a deer that they hunted every day. He was no threat to them.

While all the men were intoxicated and busy making arrangements for the ceremony, the horse walked to the ditch where the prince was held captive. He bent down on his knees and lowered his head. The reins dropped into the ditch and Indrajit held on to them tightly. The horse pulled and Indrajit sprang out. He hopped on his horse and they trotted away quietly.

At midnight the tribals came to the ditch to take Indrajit for the sacrifice, but he was not there. They lit their torches made of wood and grass, and spread out in a search, but they could not find Indrajit or the horse who, by this time, were many miles away. By crossing the jungle, the path had been shortened by many miles so that now the prince was far ahead of the army.

Jai Sri was taken to the King of Kamroop by the soldier on the same day that Indrajit entered the capital city. Indrajit stayed at an inn. The innkeeper was an old woman. She was very kind to Indrajit. She gave him good food and a very good place to stay. She kept his horse in her stable. Neither of them could understand the other's language, so it was difficult for them to communicate.

The prince was tired from traveling for so many days, so he fell asleep. That night the woman's young daughter came home after visiting a friend's house. The mother said, "A beautiful boy is staying in your room so tonight you can stay in another room."

The daughter first went to her own room and, when she saw Indrajit, she immediately fell in love with him. She had never seen such a beautiful face in her life. She went back to her mother and said, "What will you do to that boy?"

Her mother said, "The same as I did with the others!" Her daughter became very sad and left to find another place to sleep.

The old woman was a magician. Her inn business was only a trick for trapping foreigners. Her real business was selling people as slaves. By her magical powers she would change them into goats and keep them until ten to twelve were collected. She fed them grass and leaves, and then at the time of selling she would turn them back into human beings.

In the morning the old woman turned Indrajit into a goat and put him in the stable with his horse. The old woman's daughter came and asked, "Where is the boy?"

The woman said, "In the stable. After a long time I have finally found one boy. I hope it's good luck for me. Maybe now more foreigners will come," and she smiled.

The horse recognized Indrajit even though he had been changed into a goat and became very protective of him.

During the day a few soldiers of Kamroop came to the inn. They knew

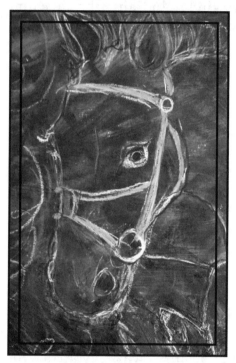

the old lady and her business very well and they said, "A prince is coming. He was riding behind us. Probably more men will be coming in search of him. If you could trap all of them, then you could make much money."

The innkeeper was very greedy. She thought, "If someone else hears about this, they will try to trap the prince first and take him to their place. I should go and find him before anyone hears the news."

She told her daughter to look after the goat and she went away to look for the prince. Her daughter said, "Mother, if a purchaser comes and offers enough money, then I will have to sell the goat. Tell me how to sell him."

The mother whispered in her ear, "As soon as you take off his collar he will become a human." The mother was in a hurry so she dressed beautifully and went out in search of the prince.

Her daughter was in love with Indrajit so as soon as her mother left, she went straight to the stable and took off the collar on the goat. The goat at once turned into the prince. As soon as he turned into human form, Indrajit leaped on his horse and galloped away. The girl ran after him, but the horse was so fast that it quickly disappeared from her sight. She was tired from running and sat down on the road and began to cry. She said to herself, "If I don't find that beautiful boy again, I will die." Then she stood up and went in search of Indrajit.

The two soldiers who were waiting by the tree finally got the horses that were sent back to them, and they began to ride toward the capital of Kamroop. On the way they saw the old innkeeper and asked her if she had seen a beautiful boy riding on a fast horse. The woman said, "Do you mean the prince?"

They both said, "Yes, the prince. Where is he?"

The woman said, "I heard that he was coming. That's why I came here to take him back with me to my inn."

The soldiers said, "Oh, no. There is no one else coming. We are the last soldiers. The prince injured us, tied us to a tree, and left. He must have reached there long ago."

The old woman said, "A boy with a horse is staying in my inn. Perhaps he is the prince. I don't understand his language but he is very beautiful."

When they heard this, the soldiers became very happy and said, "He is the prince! He is the prince! Oh beautiful lady, we will give you much money if you show us where the boy is!"

The greedy woman said, "Follow me. I'll show you. He is in my stable. His horse is there, too."

The soldiers said, "Oh no, he could run away from there! Did you lock the doors?"

The woman said, "No. But he can't run away. I turned him into a goat and my daughter is there watching him right now."

All three went back to the inn. Both soldiers drew their swords because they were afraid of Indrajit's strength. The door of the stable was closed. The old woman said, "He is inside. Go in and you will find him."

The soldiers whispered, "Don't make any noise. You open the door and then we will go inside and catch him."

The old woman angrily said, "You cowards! He is a goat. He can't do anything to you! Why are you so afraid?" She pushed open the door and found that neither the goat nor the horse were there!

The old woman thought that possibly her daughter had sold the goat, but when the woman went to her room, she saw that her daughter was not there. She was very confused and told the soldiers that either the boy had run away, or her daughter had sold him to a trader. The woman saddled her horse, and then all three rode off to search for the prince in the capital.

Indrajit was very cautious now. He realized that Kamroop was a place of magic and that anyone could trap him. He decided to go straight to the palace where he would either get killed, or be successful in bringing his sister back.

When the first soldier entered the palace with Jai Sri, the king was overwhelmed with joy. He took her in his arms and then ushered her to his room where the queen was sitting. They both hugged and kissed Jai Sri again and again and said, "My child! You were lost for so many years and now at last, by the grace of God, we have found you. We are so happy today!" The king called his ministers and ordered them to arrange a celebration to honor the safe return of the princess.

The ministers informed the public throughout the kingdom of the celebration, and the people started singing, dancing, and doing many different kinds of magic shows.

The palace was heavily decorated, and different kinds of magic shows were also set up and ready to go.

Jai Sri told the king and queen that she was not their daughter, that she was the daughter of the King of Ayodhya, but they did not believe her. They thought she wanted to go back to her husband in Ayodhya. They said, "You are our only daughter. Look, the whole kingdom is yours. If you are married to the Prince of Ayodhya, then he should come here. The marriage is not binding because he did not ask our consent. Don't be afraid. Our army is as powerful as any."

Jai Sri could not understand what they were talking about. She was very confused, so she did not say anything more.

In the outside hall, all the courtiers, generals, ministers, and their families were seated. The king, queen, and Jai Sri entered and sat down on a well-decorated throne. The musicians, dancers, and famous magicians were in the center. First the music began, and then several girls and boys in beautiful costumes started to dance.

While everyone was lost in watching the dance, Indrajit came riding in on his horse and stood in front of the king. The horse was very smart. He at once knelt down on his knees and then stood up again. The king thought it was part of the show. He started clapping, and everyone followed him.

When Jai Sri saw her brother in the court, she thought he had also been kidnapped by the soldiers. She was very frightened and screamed loudly.

The king at once stopped the show. Indrajit got down from his horse and Jai Sri ran to him and hugged him. The king thought that this must be the boy to whom she was married, and again he became very happy. He led both of them toward the throne and told them to sit down and watch the show.

The two soldiers who were looking for the prince also heard the celebration, and they thought that if they went there, they would probably find the prince hiding among the people. They told the old innkeeper that they were going to the palace to join the celebration, and she said that she also wanted to go. So all three rode toward the palace.

On the way the old woman found her daughter running barefoot, like a person who had lost her mind. She said, "What happened to you? Where are you going?"

Her daughter said, "He ran away! He ran away! I am searching for him. I love him!" The woman put her daughter on her horse, and they continued to the palace. When the four arrived, they left their horses outside and went into the hall where the music was playing.

All of them saw the prince sitting on the throne by the side of the king. The old woman's daughter could not stop herself and ran toward him like someone possessed. She climbed the steps of the throne, and hugged the prince very tightly.

The king again stopped the show, and asked the girl, "Who are you?"

The girl only said, "He ran away. He ran away. I love him! I love him!" The king could not understand all this. He thought the prince was married to his daughter, but now he saw this girl and thought she was his lover. He became very upset. He did not want his daughter with a prince who had another woman.

The king said, "Oh prince, I thought you loved my daughter and married her. I thought you would be the king after me, because I don't have a son. I have already adopted you in my mind. But I see you have another woman, and I don't want my daughter in pain."

Indrajit said, "Sire, there has been a big mistake. I am the Prince of Ayodhya and this is my sister Jai Sri. Your soldiers kidnapped her thinking that she was your daughter. To rescue my sister, I came here all the way from Ayodhya at the risk of my life. Now I want to take my sister back."

The king said, "Then where is my daughter? She was in Ayodhya!"

Indrajit said, "Sire, my older brother, whose name is Vikram, saved your daughter from the witch of Sundarban Island, and now she is married to him. She said that she was taken away by the witch when she was only three years old. Because she was lost for so many years, she thought you would not accept her again, and so she decided to live in Ayodhya. Otherwise, my brother would have brought her here to Kamroop."

The king now understood everything. He did not punish his soldiers. He said, "Prince, in my heart I have already adopted you as my son and claimant of this kingdom. Will you live with me?"

Indrajit said, "Sire, I have to take my sister to Ayodhya first. Then, yes, I will come back to you."

The king said, "And what will be the fate of this girl?"

The prince replied, "This girl saved my life. I can't forget her. Her mother turned me into a goat and she rescued me."

The king said to the girl, "What do you want as a reward for saving the life of my son?" The girl, with tears in her eyes, said, "I want nothing else. I want only him. I love him!" Then, she fainted.

The prince realized her love and took her in his arms and comforted her in various ways. When her outer awareness returned, he said, "Don't be sad. I understand your love. You saved my life. You will be with me forever as my wife, for how can I resist such love and devotion?"

The king gave his minister orders to arrange a journey to Ayodhya for himself, the queen, Jai Sri, Indrajit and the innkeeper's daughter. For the queen and the innkeeper's daughter, fast chariots were summoned, while Jai Sri, Indrajit, and the king rode on horses.

After several days journey, the group reached Ayodhya. When the King of Ayodhya found out that Indrajit and Jai Sri were both alive and had returned home safely, he was very happy. He ordered his ministers to arrange a celebration honoring their safe return.

When he heard that the King and Queen of Kamroop had also arrived to see their long lost daughter, Jivanti, he became even happier and took them with full respect to his palace where they, at last, saw their beautiful daughter.

The King of Kamroop met his son-in-law, Vikram, who was humble, kind, and also beautiful. He blessed them both. He said to the King of Ayodhya, "Dear friend, my daughter has chosen to marry your son. I don't have anyone else except my daughter. I also understand you have chosen Vikram as the heir to the throne of Ayodhya. Oh friend, in my heart I have adopted Indrajit as my son, and vowed that he be chosen heir to my kingdom. Indrajit has agreed to it. Now I humbly ask for your consent on this matter."

The King of Ayodhya said, "By trading our children in this way, we will be close friends. If Indrajit has agreed to it, then we have to accept it."

The King of Kamroop again said, "I have one last request dear friend before we leave. Will you make arrangements for the marriage ceremony of Indrajit and the beautiful girl who saved his life?"

The king happily agreed. After the celebration, the king, queen, Indrajit, and his wife all left for Kamroop. Indrajit lived there happily and ruled the kingdom well.

-O-O-O-

Early the next morning the maid servant went to Sundar's room and started singing. Sundar woke up with his mind immersed in her song. He felt very good.

When the song was completed, Sundar said, "I liked your song very much. I want you to sing everyday in the morning." The maid servant bowed to him and left to bring his breakfast.

Sundar went to the dome room as usual. He sat on his throne and began to think about Indrajit's capture by the tribals. They were really terrible people. He had heard that when they sacrificed a man to their goddess, they tied him on a board and shot arrows all through his body. Then they cut his head off and offered it to the goddess. Indrajit's horse had saved his life. Otherwise, the tribals would have killed him in this terrible way!

Sundar said to himself, "I would like to have a horse like that!"

That morning when the king came to see him, Sundar at once said, "Father, I want a horse--not an ordinary horse, but a horse that can run like a hawk, and fight with bad people."

The king said, "Dear son, you can have a horse, but it will take some time to train him. In six months though, I will give you a very beautiful horse."

Sundar was very happy thinking about the horse he would get, and he was eager to tell his friends, the fairies, about it.

That night when his parents and servants had left his room, the pigeons changed into fairies and surrounded Sundar's bed. Sundar quickly said, "Do you know, I'll get a horse in six months, a horse who can run like a hawk and can fight with enemies, just like the one Indrajit had!"

The fairies smiled and said, "Then you will not need us. You will ride your horse instead of listening to our stories."

Sundar at once said, "No, I want to hear the stories. I'll not ride the horse at night. Please, tell me what happened to Jai Sri. Did she also get married?"

All the fairies lifted the bed and flew high up in the sky. Then the eighth fairy said, "I know about Jai Sri. Listen..."

CHAPTER EIGHT

Marriage of Jai Sri

When Indrajit left for Kamroop, the king installed Vikram, his eldest son, as the King of Ayodhya. Then the old king and queen began to live as hermits in the woods.

Vikram was a good king. His subjects loved him very much, and all of his ministers and generals were faithful to him.

A few years passed and Jai Sri reached marriageable age. She was very beautiful and her brother had received several offers from the various princes of different kingdoms. He could not decide who should marry Jai Sri. So, he called his ministers and said, "I have to choose a man for my sister. Tell me how to decide which prince would be the best."

Some said, "Tally their planets." Some said, "Call them for interviews," and some said, "Let Jai Sri choose by herself."

There was an old family priest who said, "In my opinion, there must be a series of tests. The one who passes all the tests will marry Jai Sri." The rest of the ministers agreed.

The next day Vikram proclaimed that any man who was able to pass a series of tests would be the one to marry his sister. The ministers informed all kings and queens in neighboring countries. They put forth these conditions: the man should not be more than 25 years old; he should not be married; he should not be sick; and he should be from a royal family.

On the announced date, princes from different kingdoms gathered in the open area of a huge amphitheatre. The high court, other courtiers, and invited well-wishers filled the tiers of seats. The princes who had come were curious about the tests, and each one was acting as if he were the most qualified.

When each prince had taken his assigned place, the herald announced, "Oh brave princes, you all know why you are here today. Listen carefully. The great King of Ayodhya's sister, Jai Sri, who has reached her marriageable age, will be married to the man who passes all of the tests put to him. Everyone who is attending this contest to win Jai Sri's hand will get a chance to show his strength, wisdom, and skill at archery. Now, get ready for the contest!" The crowd cheered loudly.

"Over here is a chariot made completely of iron. The one who can pull it completely around this arena in five minutes will be the winner."

One by one, all the young princes tried to pull the iron chariot. A few could not even lift its yoke, and the rest could pull it only three or four steps. The herald announced, "None of you could pull the chariot. So no one is winner or loser." All the princes were happy since if one of them had succeeded, the others would have been defeated.

The herald announced the second test, "There is a bottle on the table in front of me with a long knife by its side, and a pan of water boiling on a stove. Inside the bottle there is a red apple that is bigger than the mouth of the bottle. The test is to take the apple out of the bottle, either whole or in pieces, without breaking the bottle. This is to be done within two minutes."

The contestants all walked around the table and then said, "It is not possible. No one can do it. The King of Ayodhya really doesn't want his sister to get married. That is why he has made such an impossible test!"

The herald finally said, "Since no one can think of how to take the apple out of the bottle, no one is the winner."

The contestants, who were full of ego, thinking that they would be the one to marry Jai Sri, became very upset. But, there was still one more test, so they had not lost all hope for the chance to marry her.

The herald again announced, "Listen, oh brave men. Over there is a 30-meter well. By the side of the well there is a bow and an arrow. The arrow has a hook on its head, and on the tail there is a long string. In the well there is a ring of gold fitted with a gem that shimmers in the water. Because of this light, you can see the ring very clearly. This ring fits on the finger of the princess. The one who can pierce the ring through the middle, and pull it out of the well in one minute, will put the ring on Jai Sri's finger and become her husband."

The contestants checked the well, ring, and bow and many of them did not even want to try. Only a few, who were expert in archery, went to the well to try their skill. Some of them could not pierce the ring and some others pierced it, but could not pull the 30 meters of string up in under one minute.

The herald raised both his hands and said, "It seems that there is no archer remaining in the world who can pass this test. Is there anyone else here who thinks that he can pass any of these tests? If so, please come forward now."

A tall, thin, young man, wearing only a white cotton sheet, but with a glowing face, came forward from the audience and said, "I am a prince of Magadha. I live on Bindhyachal Mountain. I heard about the contest and I came here to see it. I see that no one has passed a single test, and so I want to try." He threw his sheet on the ground and came to the center of the arena. He was wearing a loin cloth and nothing else. He went up to the chariot, filled his chest with air in a long inhalation, and then held his breath.

He then lifted the iron yoke and, breathing in a controlled way, pulled the chariot all the way around the arena in three minutes. The audience that filled the amphitheatre spontaneously clapped when he reached the finish line, seeing his amazing strength. The other contestants, however, became very angry.

The Prince of Magadha at once went over to the table and saw the bottle, knife, and the water that was boiling on a stove nearby. He looked minutely at the apple and then quickly poured the hot water into the bottle. The apple was made of wood pieces glued together and painted with red wax. As soon as the hot water filled the bottle, the apple separated into pieces and with the help of the knife the prince poured the pieces out, one by one.

The audience was again happy, seeing his deep wisdom. The audience was now very excited to see if the prince could pull the ring out of the well. The others contestants, who were now angrier, began to yell, "He is not from a royal family! He should not be allowed in the contest!"

The Prince of Magadha walked quickly to the well without caring about their shouting. He took the bow and shot the arrow through the center of the ring. He then turned and ran very fast, holding the end of the string. Within half a minute, the arrow came out of the well with the ring hanging on the hook. He lifted the ring and showed it to everyone.

When the other princes realized that the Prince of Magadha would win the contest, they became very envious and violent. They began to break and burn everything around them. The soldiers of Ayodhya immediately intervened to try and stop them. The soldiers drew their swords and a huge fight ensued. The arena turned into a battlefield.

King Vikram ordered his generals to drive out all the mischief makers. But the princes were angry and they continued to fight, trying to take Jai Sri who was sitting on a high throne, away by force.

The Prince of Magadha, the winner of the contest, had neither a sword to defend himself nor a horse to escape on. He did not want to fight but, to protect his life, he took hold of the iron chariot and when anyone tried to attack him, he pushed them away with it. When the army of Ayodhya started fighting furiously, the other princes began to run away. This gave the Prince of Magadha a chance to secretly leave the amphitheater. He passed by the throne where Jai Sri was sitting and whispered to her, "If you want peace, then come to Bindhyachal Mountain." Only Jai Sri heard his voice and saw him leaving. Then the Prince of Magadha found a horse running loose outside the amphitheater and, in one leap, he jumped on its back and rode away.

Jai Sri went to her room and changed her court robes. She left the palace dressed as a maid servant. The soldiers of Ayodhya were still driving the angry princes far away from the city. No one knew that she was gone.

When all the fighting had stopped, the soldiers came back to the capital. When Vikram returned from the battle, he went to Jai Sri's room to console her, but found she was not there. He at once came out and told his ministers that the princess had been taken away, and he sent the army out in all directions to find her. He also ordered spies be sent into other kingdoms to look for her.

When Jai Sri left the capital, she ran to the south. She knew only that the prince who had passed all the tests lived on Bindhyachal Mountain. But she was afraid that the king's soldiers would be looking for her and, if they found her, would take her back to Ayodhya. So she decided to hide during the day and to walk at night.

She found a dry well that was covered by bushes and grass. She descended into the well and hid there all day. That night she came out and continued walking to the south. She said to herself, "The prince passed all the tests, and so I am married to him. I can't marry anyone else. If I go back to the palace, then definitely the king and his ministers will try to marry me to someone else. I don't want to marry anyone else."

The Prince of Magadha had left his home when he was eight years old. His name was Ratnakar. His mother died when he was born and his father, the king, remarried. His step-mother gave birth to a son and became jealous of Ratnakar because she knew that he would be the King of Magadha some day. She was very cruel to him, so he left his home and reached Bindhyachal Mountain, where he started living in a cave.

There were saints living on Bindhyachal Mountain, and the prince started meeting them and learning about God. He found peace living in a cave, and he began to meditate every day. Slowly, he developed wisdom, love, and compassion. All the animals in the jungle became his friends.

Once while he was meditating, he saw a vision of Jai Sri in his mind and a sound came, "Ratnakar, save her! Save her!" He left his cave and went straight to Ayodhya. After the contest Ratnakar returned and began to live in the cave as before.

As Jai Sri walked she did not know how to get to Bindhyachal Mountain. She was heading south and reached a desert. She walked all night on the sand, which was still hot, and in the morning she could not find a place to hide. She saw the sand dunes rising up in front of her, and she was afraid that the soldiers on their horses might be coming at any moment. She hid behind a cluster of grass and then saw in the distance several horsemen coming toward her very quickly. She could not think of what to do. Nearby, there was a dead horse lying on the sand. Vultures had eaten all its intestines. Jai Sri slowly crawled toward the horse. The stench was great, but she did not care, and entered inside the carcass.

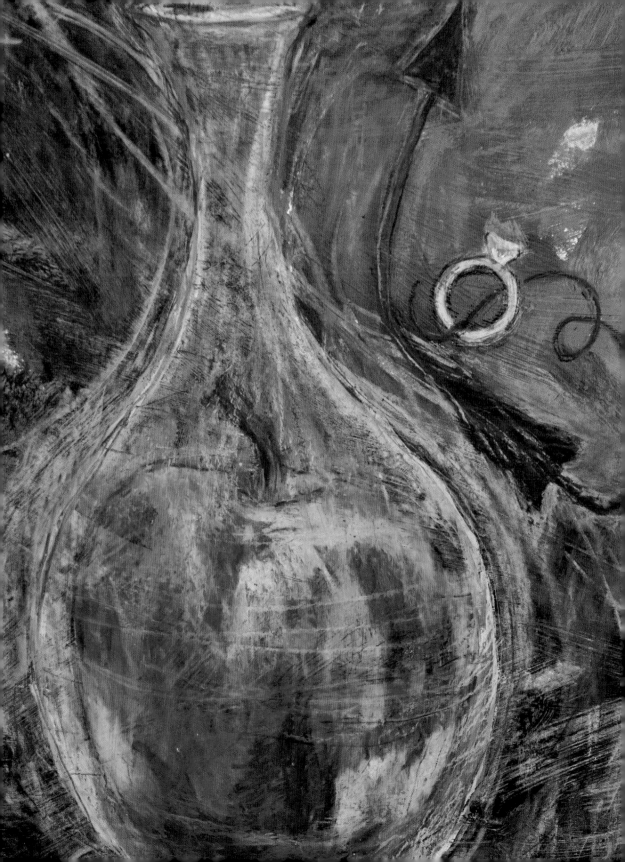

The horsemen saw something moving ahead and sped up their horses. But, when they reached the place, they saw that no one was there. They looked all around and then went near the dead horse. The smell was so strong that they could not stand it and decided to head back to the palace.

Jai Sri came out when she realized that no one was there any longer. She was very thankful to God who had created a shelter for her protection. She thought she should put the horse in a grave as a mark of respect. Her eyes went to the saddle and she saw a folded paper wedged in the stirrup. It was a letter on which was written, "If you want peace, then come to Bindhyachal." There was also a rough map showing the mountain.

Jai Sri at once realized that it was her husband's horse, and it had died here somehow. She thought, "He put this letter on the saddle in case I found the horse."

Jai Sri, without wasting any more time, started walking. The soldiers had already come and gone so she was not afraid, but it was still a long way to walk, and the path was full of dangers. The letter, though, strengthened her faith, and determination.

The heat of the sun burnt her skin. The sweat and dirt made her hair hang in stringy locks. The smell of the horse was in her clothes. She had the appearance of a walking ghost.

She crossed the desert and went into the woods. Walking in the woods was much better; at least there was shade, animals, birds, and water to wash with and drink. After washing herself, Jai Sri was tired so she rested in the shade of a tree. She saw some goats grazing on the leaves of bushes, and she saw a woman trying to drive several other goats. The goats were running away, and it was very difficult for the woman to handle so many goats all alone.

When the woman saw someone sitting under a tree she said, "Will you help me, please? I want to get these goats on the road."

Jai Sri stood up and began to help the woman, who gave her a bamboo stick and said, "I'll go in the front of the goats and you drive them from behind."

Jai Sri, without saying anything, obeyed her. For three days they walked in the jungle. At night they would rest under a tree, or by the side of the river. In these three days they became close friends. The woman was also going to the mountains, so it was good company for Jai Sri, and, with the goats, no one would suspect her identity.

After walking for several more days, they reached the bottom of Bindhyachal Mountain where there was flat land full of thorny bushes, the favorite food of goats. There were also berries, papayas, and bananas nearby in the jungle.

The woman was acquainted with every corner of this place. She cleaned a large, dry cave that had an open area for sitting near its mouth. Both women began to live there.

Vikram and his ministers thought that one of the princes had kidnapped Jai Sri, so the soldiers disguised themselves and went to different kingdoms looking for her. One year passed and all the soldiers returned to the capital and informed the king that Jai Sri could not be found. Vikram lost hope and decided not to send any more people in search of his sister.

When summer was over, the goat woman said that she would take her goats to the north. She wanted Jai Sri to go with her, but Jai Sri said, "I will stay here in the cave for a longer time, then I will go to the other side of the mountain."

The goat woman gave Jai Sri a goat for milk and left for the north. Jai

Sri remained alone in the cave. By living in the woods for such a long time she became accustomed to it and had no fear at all. She would take the goat for grazing to different places. Actually, all the time she was looking for Ratnakar. In this way a year passed, but she could not find him.

The goat woman came back the next summer and lived with Jai Sri. She again left for the north when winter started. The time was gradually passing and Jai Sri began to think that probably the prince had forgotten her, or that he only wanted her to be on this mountain to attain peace. Her life was simple, and she was happy, but she was still expecting the prince to appear at any moment.

In six years Jai Sri had totally changed. She was completely dark, with lines on her face highlighting her high cheek bones. She was wearing a rough hand-made cloth that was given to her by the goat woman. Her uncombed hair was hanging in locks. She was strong, hardy, and rough in speech.

After handing over the reign of the kingdom to Vikram, the old king and queen had decided to visit all the holy places and temples of India. They dressed as hermits and left for the pilgrimage on foot. On the way they met other people who were also traveling to visit holy places. All the pilgrims began to travel together, which made it safe for everyone.

The pilgrims headed to the east where the sacred river Ganges meets the ocean. Then they took the ocean coast and went toward the south end of India and, from there, they climbed over to the west coast.

After visiting temples on the west coast, the old king and queen left the crowd and went to visit Bindhyachal Mountain. They had heard that several high saints lived there and they wanted to meet them. At the bottom of the mountain the land was flat and the jungle was very thick. A small trail led through the jungle and then went straight up to the top of the mountain. The king and queen took this trail and reached the base of the mountain.

Suddenly, they heard the noise of the breaking of trees and they thought that it was the wood-cutters who lived in the area. The king coughed so that these people would know that someone was coming. In an instant, a herd of wild elephants surrounded them on all sides and from the mountain side a huge tusked elephant blocked the trail!

The king said to the queen, "Now, it's the end of our journey. Remember almighty God. These elephants will kill us, no doubt!" The tusked elephant screamed very loudly, and all the other elephants began to break the trees and kick the ground with their front legs.

A saint who was living in a cave a little higher up on the mountain heard the elephant noises and immediately came out of his cave. The elephants were just then preparing to attack. The saint ran down the trail and stood directly in front of the tusked elephant. He put his fingers to his mouth and whistled very loudly. At once all the elephants dispersed into the jungle.

The king and queen bowed to the saint who said, "This place is not safe for two people alone. Pilgrims visit here only in big caravans so that the elephants will not attack them."

The king said, "Reverend Sir, you are very merciful. You saved our lives. I thought that our journey in life was ended, that we would be killed by these elephants. But, God has saved us through you."

The saint said, "Now there is no danger. This trail you are on goes up to the top of the mountain where you will find a temple. On the way you will see several caves where different saints are living. From the top, the trail goes down the other side of the mountain and you will find flat land there, full of thorny bushes. That jungle is also safe. You will meet goat herders there and you can get milk, fruits, and different kinds of edible roots from them."

The king said, "I invite you to visit us in Ayodhya."

The saint said, "If God wishes."

The king and queen took the trail and slowly reached the temple on top of the mountain. From there they could see the whole flat land below, stretching out for several miles. They were tired and so they stayed at the temple for a few days. When they were refreshed by rest and the cool mountain air, they started on their journey again. They reached the bottom of the other side of the mountain in the evening, after the sun had set, and it was getting dark.

The king was looking for a place to stay the night. He heard the noise of a goat and they both walked in that direction. After going a short distance, they found a cave from where the sound of the goat was coming.

The king said, "Is there anyone in this cave? We are pilgrims."

A woman came out and looked at them and said, "Come in." There was no light in the cave. The woman gave them a place near the goat to sleep overnight. She also gave them milk and fruits to eat. The king and queen were tired and so, after eating, they both fell asleep.

In the morning the woman woke up. She went to fetch water for the pilgrims to wash. When she came back with the water, they were both talking. The woman gave them the water. When she realized they were talking about Ayodhya, her old memories revived. She said, "Are you from Ayodhya?" And then she recognized them. She thought, "My brother has not come and probably he will not come. God has sent my parents. Probably God wants me to go back with them. They are old now and I can serve them."

She bowed to the king and queen and said, "Do you recognize me?"

They said, "No, we have never met you before. We have come to this place for the first time. Who are you?"

The woman said, "I am your daughter, Jai Sri!"

The king and queen were shocked to hear this and could not believe her.

Jai Sri realized that they did not recognize her so she started telling them the story of Vikram; how he was kidnapped by the witch, how she was also kidnapped by the soldiers of Kamroop, and how Indrajit had brought her back. She told them about the marriage tests, and how the princes fought, and how she finally ran away from Ayodhya.

When the king and queen heard all this, their tears began to fall and they both hugged her tightly. They felt much pain to see her living like a destitute person in a cave. Jai Sri said, "You should not feel pain. It was all destined. I am in much peace here."

The queen said, "My child, I can't leave you here now. Either go back with us to Ayodhya, or we will also live here with you."

Jai Sri thought that if she didn't go back to Ayodhya, then her parents would have to stay in the cave with her, and it would be very hard for them to live this kind of life. So she said, "Mother, don't worry. I'll go with you. You both are old, and I will be honored to serve you with love."

The king collected their things and all three of them, together with the goat, started for Ayodhya. Jai Sri was well acquainted with the path and in a few days they reached home.

When Vikram heard that Jai Sri was alive and had been found by the old king and queen, he became very happy and went to his parents' place to see them. After six years' separation, brother and sister met again. Vikram made a hut for Jai Sri near their parents and all three began to live happily.

Jai Sri had done hard austerities for six years so now she did not feel any difficulty in serving her parents. They were also leading a very simple life, and all three were in much peace together.

Six months later, when winter was over, Ratnakar decided to travel to the north. He remembered that the old King of Ayodhya had invited him to visit there. On an auspicious day, he started his journey. After visiting different holy places in the north, he went to Ayodhya where the old king and queen were living.

The king and queen immediately recognized the saint and bowed to his feet. He was their life saver. They took him to their house and gave him a high seat on which to rest.

Jai Sri came to visit her parents and saw them sitting at the feet of a tall, thin man whose face was glowing like the sun. She came near them and sat down. The king said, "Jai Sri, this saint saved our lives. Bow to him." Jai Sri bent down at the man's feet. The saint lifted her up and took a ring from his bag and put it on her finger.

The king and queen were surprised to see the saint putting a ring on their daughter's finger, but Jai Sri recognized the prince and said, "This is the man for whom I waited for six years in a cave, but who never came."

Ratnakar said, "I always knew that you were living in a cave on the other side of the mountain, but I wanted you to do hard austerities to attain peace. Jai Sri, in our past life we were together. You were my disciple. To bring you back to the feet of the Lord, I came to the contest. Our marriage is not physical. We are married to God."

When Vikram found out that a saint had come to visit his parents, he came to his parents' place. He also recognized the saint. He was the only prince who passed all of the three tests. He said, "By passing those tests, you are married to Jai Sri. Now I want to give half of my kingdom to Jai Sri and you."

Ratnakar said, "Vikram, you are my brother now. I don't want wealth or property. I am in peace, and I want to remain in peace. Jai Sri is my wife, my disciple. We are always together in God. If she wants to accept half the kingdom, then she can stay here, but I have to go back to my own place."

Jai Sri bowed to her parents and brother and said, "I am going with him where I belong." Ratnakar and Jai Sri left for Bindhyachal Mountain and never came to the city again.

-○○○-

The fairy, after finishing the story, said, "Now, Sundar, go to sleep." Sundar tried to go to sleep but he could not. As soon as he closed his eyes he would see Jai Sri and Ratnakar walking in the jungles. He said, "Oh fairies, tonight I am not getting sleep." The fairies swung the bed gently, but he could not sleep at all. It was morning and the fairies brought the bed back to Sundar's room.

One of the fairies said, "Sundar, if you don't get sleep at night, then you will be sleepy all day and your parents will guess that you aren't getting any sleep at night. They will worry about you."

While the fairies were talking to Sundar, the maid servant came to the door and heard voices. She thought that one of the other maid servants wanted to take her place. She became jealous and secretly opened the door. As soon as the door opened, the nine fairies turned back into pigeons.

The maid servant came in and said, "Sundar, I heard someone talking to you."

Sundar said, "Oh, I could not sleep at all last night. Probably I was talking to myself."

When the maid servant heard this, she went to the king and said, "Sire, early this morning I went to the door of Prince Sundar and heard someone talking. But, when I opened the door, no one was there. The prince said that he could not sleep last night."

The king and queen at once went to Sundar's room and asked, "What happened? Why didn't you sleep? We are worried about you. Are you sick? What is the matter?"

Sundar said, "I am alright. I just couldn't sleep last night, that's all. I want to go to sleep now. Today I'll not sit in the dome."

The king said, "Take a good rest. You don't need to sit in the dome every day." They left the room and Sundar fell asleep.

The king became suspicious and said to the queen, "I think someone is going to Sundar's room, and he is afraid to tell us." He ordered all the maid servants to secretly watch through the crack of the door, to see if anyone was coming to his room at night.

CHAPTER NINE

Our Story

That night Sundar was as excited as ever to listen to a new story. When everyone left his room, he waited for the fairies to come as usual. But they did not come. He said, "Oh fairies, why don't you come? Are you angry with me? Do you not want to tell me any more stories?" But the fairies neither appeared nor answered.

Sundar became very upset and in a loud voice he said, "If you don't come, then I'll leave the room!" He pretended to leave the room. One of the maid servants was watching him through a crack in the door. She at once moved away so that Sundar would not know that someone was watching him.

Just as Sundar was about to open the door, one of the fairies, the fairy leader, whispered, "Sundar, don't leave the room. I will tell you a story, but not now. You have to wait for some time. We can't appear just now."

Sundar lay on his bed and waited and waited for them, but no one appeared. He whispered, "Oh fairies, are you sleeping? Why don't you come? I am waiting for you!"

When the maid servant, who was spying from outside, finally fell asleep, all nine fairies appeared. The head fairy said, "Sundar, we must be very alert now. Your servants are watching you. Don't make any noise." They silently lifted the bed and flew high up in the sky.

The head fairy said, "Sundar, you slept all day long. Now you will not get any sleep tonight. Tomorrow, your parents will again say, 'Why don't you get any sleep? What is wrong with you?' So, can you get some sleep tonight, and then tomorrow I'll tell you a story?"

Sundar said, "All right. I'll try." The fairies swung his bed gently and he fell asleep. The fairies silently brought his bed back down and changed into pigeons.

The maid servant watched all night but saw nothing. In the morning the one chosen maid servant went to Sundar's room and started singing. Sundar opened his eyes and said, "Oh, I slept for a long time. I didn't even dream. I feel very good today."

He took a bath and met his parents. He then went to the dome room where he could be seen by all.

His father was very happy to see Sundar acting grown up and decided to arrange for his education. He went to the dome and sat with him and said, "My dear son, you are growing up now and I think you should go to school. Everyone in the kingdom has already seen you many times. They don't need to see you in the dome any more. Starting the day after tomorrow, the maid servants will take you to school where you will learn reading, writing, archery, and how to ride a horse. Also, there will be other boys your age with whom you can play. In the evening, you will come back home."

Sundar was very excited about school. He said, "Father, I would really love to go to school. Does this mean that I may now have my own horse? I could ride him to school!"

The king said, "You will be given a horse to ride to school, but you will not get your very own horse for six months." The king left the dome and called his minister to arrange schooling for the prince.

That night, after the king and queen had left Sundar's room, the fairies appeared. The maid servants were not expecting anyone to come to the room since there was no one there the night before, but they had to watch the whole night anyway. It was the king's order.

When Sundar saw the fairies, he became very excited and said, "Day after tomorrow, I am going to school and I will get to ride on a horse to get there!"

The head fairy whispered, "Speak in a low voice, Sundar. Someone may hear you. We will take you up into the sky. We can't talk here." They took the bed up and away into the sky.

The head fairy said, "This is our story. Listen."

We are fairies of heaven where the King of the Gods rules. His name is Indra. He is a most powerful, strong, beautiful, and wise king. But, he has much pride, being the King of Gods, and he has a great fear of losing his kingdom.

In Indra's palace, the walls and ceilings are made of gold with many precious jewels embedded in them. The curtains are made of silk with embroidery of gold and silver threads. The chairs and tables are made of pure sandalwood, carved in different shapes. Celestial musicians sing all day and night, and celestial dancers dance in the air.

Indra is all-powerful but still he is very watchful of human beings. He is afraid that his position may some day be taken over by a human being who develops great virtue. For that reason, he disturbs those human beings who are on the path of virtue.

We nine fairies were his spies. If he received information that a certain human being was doing hard austerities to find the One Supreme God, he would send us to that person to charm them with our beauty and music. In this way, the person's mind would get distracted from meditation on God, and get caught again by desire for the world.

King Indra, though, is very kind-hearted too. If the person does get caught in desire for the world, he makes that person a king or queen of some country in your world so that they may enjoy all worldly pleasures.

Long, long ago, a king named Dharma Setu was the ruler of Ayodhya. He was young, brave, strong, and very handsome. He was only thirteen years old when he became king.

Dharma Setu ruled for ten years. Through his bravery and virtues, he extended his kingdom in many directions. Once, while he was on the battlefield where furious fighting was taking place, a pigeon who was being chased by a hawk fell down on the ground out of fear. The king saw that his army was moving straight toward the place where the pigeon had dropped and he said to himself, "Oh, innocent bird, you will now be crushed by my army."

A huge elephant was running in front of the army. As soon as he came near the pigeon, the chain of the huge bell that was hanging on his neck broke, and the bell fell down right over the pigeon, protecting him from being crushed.

The king saw all this happening right before his very own eyes and said to himself, "Why am I fighting for more land? God is taking care of everything. He saved the pigeon from the hawk by dropping him to the ground, and then He saved him from being crushed by dropping a bell over him."

Dharma Setu at once stopped the battle and told his ministers to return all the villages they had conquered. The following day, he gave his kingdom to his younger brother and disappeared.

Several years passed, during which time no one heard anything about King Dharma Setu. He had gone to the Himalayas where he became a hermit. He started living in the hollowed out trunk of a huge tree.

He wore only a loin cloth. He ate fruits and vegetables and, later, would only eat leaves from the trees. He would meditate day and night, praying to God to give him devotion.

King Indra was sitting on his celestial throne in heaven when, all of a sudden, it began to shake. He stood up, looking very afraid, and said to us, "Listen, there is someone in the lower worlds who is doing hard austerities. If these austerities melt the heart of Supreme God, then God will remove me and put this person in my place. Go at once and find out who this person is and where this person dwells."

All nine of us flew from heaven and searched on many different planets. We could find no one who was doing austerities of such magnitude that they could shake our king's palace. Then we flew down to your earth and, in searching from one end to the other, finally found a very thin man sitting inside a tree trunk. We guessed that he was the man who was doing the hard austerities. We did not talk to him or even appear in front of him, but quickly flew back to heaven to inform our king.

When Indra heard about the man he closed his eyes and for a few minutes remained silent. He then opened his eyes and said, "I can see him. He is King Dharma Setu. He became a hermit and now his name is Kapinjar. He is doing very hard austerities and has much devotion for God. If he can control all his sensual desires, then no doubt he will replace me. Oh fairies, go down to the earth and charm the hermit Kapinjar with your beauty, music, and sensual dances. Create lust in his mind. When he is completely overpowered by you, then bring him here and I will give him a reward for his austerities by making him the most powerful king of that planet, the King of Ayodhya, in his next life."

We bowed to King Indra and left for earth. On the way we discussed how to appear in front of Sage Kapinjar. He was living in a tree trunk with his eyes closed and he was eating only dry leaves blown inside the cave by the wind. There was no reason for him to come out, but we went there anyway and started playing, singing, and dancing. For several days we stayed there making noises, trying to distract him, but he had not a thought for the outside world.

We decided to dress as young students and go to him with the request that he give us knowledge of God. Probably then he would talk to us, and we could find a way to distract him.

We all dressed as young boys, took scriptures in our hands, and went to Sage Kapinjar. He was still sitting in the tree trunk with his eyes closed.

We started chanting "Om" in a musical voice and the sage soon opened his eyes. He said, "Who are you young students? What do you want?"

I said, "Reverend Sir, we are looking for a sage to give us knowledge of God. When we arrived in this jungle, we saw you sitting in this tree-cave, so we came to ask you to give us this knowledge."

Sage Kapinjar said, "I am happy to see young students so eager to find God. Come to this place every day and make your mind calm. Then meditate on the light of knowledge inside your mind, at the place just inside and behind the forehead. In this way, some day you will find the knowledge of God within you."

We started going to the sage every day and began to meditate. After some time, due to the sage's purity, we forgot our duty to our king and began to enjoy meditating.

Several days passed and, when we did not return to heaven, King Indra became upset. He sat down and concentrated on the earth. He saw us meditating with the sage. He became very angry and immediately came down to earth on his beautiful throne.

As soon as we saw him sitting on his throne in front of us, we remembered our duty and our real form appeared.

King Indra angrily said, "You could not drag this sage into lust, anger, or greed. Instead, you have all become hermits yourselves! It seems certain that this sage will take my place!"

The sage heard us talking and looked outside. He saw us as beautiful fairies, and he saw the king. Probably he thought that we were Indra's queens. He remembered about his being a king in the past. For a moment, the desire to be a king again popped into his mind. He at once said, "Who are you all?"

I said, "Reverend Sir, we are fairies of our king, Indra, King of the Gods,

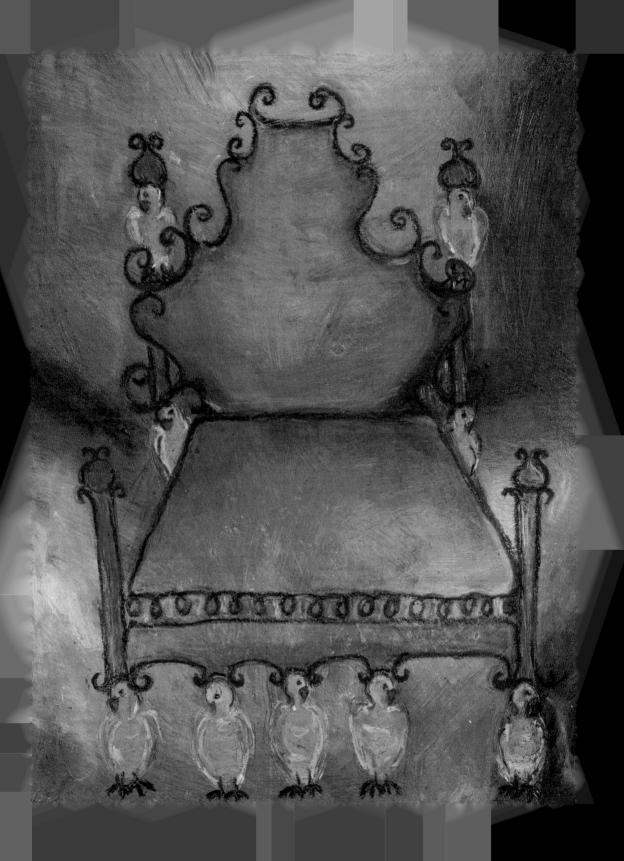

who is here in front of you."

The sage at once said, "Oh, you were disguised as young students. Now I understand why you came here. I can't be angry with any of you, but neither can I change destiny. As a punishment for trying to trick me into lust, anger, and fear, Indra will take birth as the King of Ayodhya and you nine fairies will remain on earth disguised as pigeons. Once someone on earth sees you and knows of your existence, then you can go back to heaven. As long as Indra remains on earth, I will have to do the work of Indra. I don't want to be Indra, but it is all destined. It is a punishment for me because the little desire to become king popped up in my mind for a second, when I saw your beauty."

As soon as the sage stopped talking, the earth shook very hard and he disappeared. The mountains began to fall and the waves of the ocean began to swallow the earth. The fairies jumped to protect the throne, but after lifting it on their heads, they became buried in the earth along with the throne. In a few minutes everything was finished. The whole earth became a lump of round mud and everything was buried in it.

Over thousands of years, the sun dried up the lump of mud and it cracked. The cracks filled with water and made oceans, seas, and lakes. In some places the mud clumps rose up and turned into mountains.

Slowly, a new creation started. The mountains were covered by trees, bushes, and grass. The flat lands in some places were covered by grains, and in other places by fruit trees and vegetables. Animals took birth in the jungles. Fish, crocodiles, seals, whales, and millions of other creatures took birth in the waters. Many different kinds of birds began to fly in the sky.

In the jungles, lions, tigers, elephants, deer, apes, monkeys, and human beings began to live. Those who were weak could not survive. Those who were intelligent began to live together for protection against their enemies.

Human beings were the most intelligent among all living beings. They began to live together, and to tame the animals that were fit for their use, like horses, dogs, cows, elephants, and camels.

The people separated into tribes and each tribe began to fight for land and power. In this way, the earth was divided into different countries, which human beings began to rule.

In this new creation, a kingdom was formed, named Ayodhya. It was in exactly the same place it had been in the previous creation. The former king of heaven, Indra, whose name was now Shanti Ratha, became the king of the new Ayodhya.

Although Shanti Ratha was a human being, he remembered that he had been Indra, the King of Heaven. Now he was the most powerful king on earth. By his might and wisdom, he conquered all countries and became the sole monarch of the earth.

Shanti Ratha ruled the earth for hundreds of years, but he always remembered that one day he would get his real place back in heaven. One day, he called his ministers and installed his son Prajapati as King of Ayodhya. Then he left his kingdom and went to the Himalayas to worship almighty God.

For several years Shanti Ratha worshipped God and performed hard austerities. Finally, God became pleased with him and offered him his place again as King Indra in heaven.

The fairy said, "Sundar, do you know who Prajapati was? Let us go back to your room and then I'll tell you the rest of the story." The fairies flew down into Sundar's room and surrounded his bed on all sides.

The fairy continued, "You are from the same dynasty as Prajapati, who was a brave, powerful, and intelligent king like his father Shanti Ratha."

Sundar at once said, "When Shanti Ratha became Indra again in heaven, what happened to Sage Kapinjar? He was also Indra there. Were there two Indras then?"

The fairy smiled and said, "No. Sage Kapinjar was a very pure soul, but when the desire to be king again popped into his mind, it broke his meditation. He was punished for that, working hard as Indra and living in luxuries. He remained unattached to all desires even though he was in heaven. When Shanti Ratha came back as Indra, Sage Kapinjar turned into a star, far, far away from heaven."

Once Prajapati ordered a fort to be built. The laborers dug all the high land to make it flat. While they were digging, they found this sandalwood throne. King Prajapati brought it to his palace and decorated his living room with it. The same throne was owned by many kings of your dynasty."

"You are the first person in the family who ever used this throne as a bed. No one else ever sat on this throne. We wanted you to use it because you are the most beautiful prince in the whole world, and we love you."

The maid servant who was spying outside the door heard someone talking in Sundar's room. She at once went to inform the king and queen. The king and the queen hurriedly came from the palace and dashed into Sundar's room. They saw the nine fairies surrounding the prince's bed. They stood watching them, wonderstruck! All of a sudden the fairies flapped their wings and Sundar jumped into his father's arms. The sandalwood bed began to glow. The fairies lifted it up saying, "Dear Sundar, good-bye forever!" And they disappeared into the sky.

The king and queen watched them disappear and could not understand what was happening.

Was it a dream,

or was it real?

Who were those beautiful fairies?

Only Sundar knew.

But, he kept it a secret.

ABOUT THE
Author
Leaving home at the age of eight, living in the jungles in the Kumaon region of northern India, and meeting people from all walks of life from all parts of the world, Baba Hari Dass has extensive life experience that informs his many stories for both children and adults. A life-long yogi, Babaji has never lost touch with the enchantment of being a child, skillfully weaving lessons into the stories he writes.

ABOUT THE
Illustrator
Linda Sudha Bracanovich received a Minor in Fine Arts from Michigan State University, and continued her studies in New York City at the School of Visual Arts, Parsons, and National Academy of Design, along with tutelage received from gifted artists and art history scholars, including Henry Geldzahler. Linda's primary focus these days is on practicing the 'art' of yoga, and she finds daily inspiration in the deeds, words, and unconditional love of Baba Hari Dass. The illustrations for Pigeon Throne were created using oil stick and oil pastels, each drawing inspired by these beautiful stories is an expression of devotion.

PUBLISHER'S NOTE:
Sri Rama Foundation
is a non-profit, charitable corporation founded to publish the writings of Baba Hari Dass. When the first book was published in 1975, Babaji would not accept money, having always lived his life with a vow of poverty. He requested instead that eventual profits from book sales be used to support destitute and orphaned children in India. Sri Ram Orphanage in northern India, established in 1984, fulfills this purpose. Babaji understands the needs of homeless children, and has chosen to dedicate his writings to them.